Archie Greene
and the
Magician's Secret

Archie Greene
and the
Magician's Secret

D. D. Everest

HARPER
An Imprint of HarperCollinsPublishers

Library of Congress Cataloging-in-Publication Data
Everest, D. D., author.
Archie Greene and the magician's secret / D. D. Everest. — First U.S. edition.
pages cm
Summary: Archie Greene has lived with his grandmother since he was a baby, but
when a mysterious package arrives on his twelfth birthday with instructions to take
it to a strange bookshop in Oxford, he finds himself involved with a secret society of
people who protect the world's magical books, and discovers that he has family he
never knew about.
ISBN 978-0-06-231211-2 (hardcover)
1. Magic—Juvenile fiction. 2. Books—Juvenile fiction. 3. Bookstores—England—
Oxford—Juvenile fiction. 4. Orphans—Juvenile fiction. 5. Families—England—
Oxford—Juvenile fiction. 6. Oxford (England)—Juvenile fiction. [1. Magic—Fiction.
2. Books—Fiction. 3. Secret societies—Fiction. 4. Orphans—Fiction. 5. Families—
Fiction. 6. Oxford (England)—Fiction. 7. England—Fiction.] I. Title.
PZ7.1.E94Ar 2015   2014030714
[Fic]—dc23   CIP
                                                                             AC

Typography by Carla Weise
15 16 17 18 19   CG/RRDH   10 9 8 7 6 5 4 3 2 1
❖
First U.S. edition, 2015
Originally published in the U.K. by Faber and Faber, 2014

For my parents, who taught me
that anything is possible.

And for the ones who heard it first.

Contents

The Three Types of Magic

Natural Magic

The purest kind of magic comes from magical creatures and plants and the elemental forces of nature, such as the sun, the stars, and the seas.

Mortal Magic

is man-made magic. It includes the magical instruments and other devices created by magicians to channel magical power.

Supernatural Magic

The third and darkest type of magic uses the power of spirits and other supernatural beings.

The Three Apprentice Skills

Finding

Binding

Minding

The Five Lores of Magic

In 1666, a magical accident caused the Great Fire of London. The Lores of Magical Restraint were agreed upon to prevent another magical disaster. (Lores is the magical spelling of laws.)

FIRST LORE: All magical books and artifacts must be returned to the Museum of Magical Miscellany for inspection and classification. (They are classified as level one, two, or three in magical power.)

SECOND LORE: Magical books and artifacts may not be used or bought and sold until properly identified and classified.

THIRD LORE: The unauthorized use of magic outside of magical premises is prohibited.

FOURTH LORE: The hoarding of magical books and

artifacts to accumulate personal power is outlored under the prohibition of dangerous practices.

FIFTH LORE: The mistreatment of magical creatures is expressly forbidden.

Buried deep in caverns cold
A secret that remains untold
Two ancient sentries guard the prize
With lion heart and eagle eyes.

In stony silence shadows sleep
The final gift is safe to keep
To pass requires a simple test
Name the one whom I served best.

CHAPTER 1

The Birthday Cake for No One

Sardines. That was the mystery ingredient in Loretta Foxe's chocolate cake, and both her children knew it. This particular cake was covered with blueberry icing and had twelve candles on it. It was sitting on the kitchen table in the Foxe family's house in Oxford.

As well as the cake, there were heaped piles of sandwiches; bowls of colorful chips; and a number of small, unmarked glass jars, their contents uncertain because their labels had long since peeled off. In the middle of the table stood a large jug containing a bubbly pink liquid.

Bramble and Thistle Foxe sat staring hungrily at the food laid out before them.

"Can we start now, Mum?" Bramble asked.

She was fourteen years old, with green eyes and long, dark hair that fell in thick curls down her back, and even though it was warm summer, she wore a patterned woolen hat with a pom-pom hanging over one shoulder.

"Not yet, Bramble," called Loretta Foxe, from inside the walk-in larder. Her voice vibrated with energy.

"But we're starving," groaned Thistle Foxe. He was eleven and had tousled brown hair and a smattering of dark freckles across his nose.

"Thistle, I told you to wait," Loretta insisted.

Silence.

"Well, can we have a drink at least?" asked Thistle.

"A drink?" trilled his mother. "Of course you may have a drink, my darlings! The elderberry squash is very good, but use it sparingly. We're not made of elderberry squash, you know."

Thistle Foxe rolled his eyes—the universal sign for annoying parents.

Bramble poured two glasses of elderberry squash from the large jug. The children slurped it down in one go. She picked up the jug to pour some more. At that moment Loretta emerged from the larder. A small woman with piercing turquoise eyes and a thick mane of dark hair, she wore a purple dress and was carrying another plate of sandwiches.

She caught sight of her daughter poised with the jug. "Now what did I tell you about the elderberry squash, Bramble? Do you think elderberries grow on trees?"

"No, Mum," her daughter sighed, rolling her eyes as Thistle had done.

Bramble sniffed the cake and raised her eyebrows.

"Is it your usual recipe, Mum?" Thistle asked.

"Yes," declared Loretta. "Chocolate and marshmallow, with sardine filling."

The children had guessed correctly. They knew their mother specialized in unusual combinations of food. In fact, she specialized in unusual just about everything, like the rest of the family. To the dismay of her rather stodgy neighbors, it included her taste in exterior decor. Loretta liked purple. The Foxes' front door was painted a fulsome fuchsia, and their window frames were a magnificent magenta. But what really ruffled feathers and twitched curtains on Houndstooth Road, Oxford, was that the exterior of number thirty-two was painted a bright, juicy shade of plum.

"We are celebrating a birthday," declared Loretta, placing the sandwiches on the table with a flourish.

"We can see that," said Thistle, "but whose?"

"Never you mind whose," said Loretta. "Just be glad that we are celebrating it at all."

"But a birthday cake for no one?" Bramble asked.

"I didn't say it was for no one!" Loretta sniffed, suddenly looking teary-eyed.

Bramble and Thistle exchanged concerned glances.

"Now," continued Loretta, "we just need your father. Then we can light the candles and make a toast."

"A toast to who?" asked Thistle curiously.

"You mean a toast to *whom*," corrected his mother.

"Who. Whom. Whatever." Thistle shrugged.

Loretta gave her son a dark look—a look she had perfected over many years of parenting. Then she broke into a smile like a burglar might break into a jewelry shop.

"To absent relatives, that's to whom! And to special birthdays!"

CHAPTER 2

An Unexpected Parcel

A hundred miles away in a small seaside town called West Wittering, Horace Catchpole opened the gate to number three, Crabgate Cottages. Horace was in his mid-forties and had the sort of face that wouldn't be noticed in a crowd. This was just as well, because he had the sort of job that required discretion. Horace worked for Folly & Catchpole, the oldest and most secretive law firm in England, and today he was on important business.

Clutched in his right hand was a package wrapped in plain brown parchment and secured with several pieces of leather twine. A scroll tied with a scarlet ribbon went with the package and was tucked in Horace's inside pocket for safekeeping.

Horace had no idea what was in the package, but that was not abnormal in his line of work. The London offices of Folly & Catchpole, just off Fleet Street, contained all sorts of secrets—many of them were unknown even to the longest-serving staff. The firm's reputation was built on minding its own business.

To say that Horace wasn't curious about what was in this particular package, though, would be untrue. For the last four hundred years it had been stored in the firm's cellars, waiting to be delivered on a certain date. Finally, that day had arrived, and Horace, to his great pride, had been entrusted with the job.

Horace knew the entry in the client logbook by heart. "Arrived May 10, 1603, one medium-sized package with accompanying scroll. To be brought to Mr. Archie Greene." Yet who had left the instruction was a mystery. No matter how many times Horace stared at the logbook, the name was too smudged and faded to decipher.

Horace straightened the starched cuffs of his crisply pressed but tatty shirt and buttoned the jacket of his shabby three-piece suit. He tightened his faded navy-blue tie a notch and tucked his freshly laundered handkerchief into his top pocket. Then he gave the door of number three, Crabtree Cottages two sharp knocks.

A young boy opened the door. He was small and wiry with mousy brown hair. What Horace noticed about him, though, was the color of his eyes. One was emerald green like the deepest lake, and the other was a silvered gray, the color of weathered oak.

Horace smiled benignly at the boy. He had waited a long time for this moment. He was about to speak when the boy looked up at him and said, "No thanks, we don't want any."

"Young man," Horace said, in his most self-important voice, "I am from Folly and Catchpole, the oldest law firm in England, and I am on important business."

But his words were greeted by a loud *thwack* as the door closed in his face. Horace, feeling cheated out of what was to be his crowning achievement, banged on the door again. To his surprise, it opened with such force that he nearly tumbled inside.

"Look," said the same slight boy Horace had encountered a moment ago, "I don't mean to be rude or anything, but whatever it is you're selling, we've already got one."

Horace felt his stomach twist in knots. He had thought about this moment many times. In his mind's eye, the incredulous recipient of the package would be overcome with emotion and declare that the name of Folly & Catchpole would live long in legend. But this young boy seemed completely indifferent. His parents would know better. Horace cleared his throat.

"Now, young man," he said, forcing a smile onto his lips, "is your father at home?"

The boy shook his head.

"Er . . . mother?"

"No," the boy replied. "I haven't got a father or a mother, just a gran. And she says I'm not to talk to strangers." The door closed again.

Horace wiped his brow with his handkerchief. He noticed that the handkerchief had begun to wilt.

He took a deep breath and counted to ten before knocking once more. This time the door opened only a crack.

"You again?"

"Now then," Horace said. "I am on important business—important *official* business," he added for extra effect. "I've got a parcel to deliver to this address."

The boy's expression suddenly changed.

"Why didn't you say so?" He beamed. "It's my birthday. I'm twelve today, so it must be for me."

Horace blinked uncertainly. "No, I don't think so. This package is of a very serious nature and certainly not meant for a child. . . ."

But it was too late. The boy had already grabbed the package with both hands, given it a sharp tug, and pulled it inside the house, while Horace, who was thrown off balance, fell into a clump of stinging nettles in the front garden.

By the time Horace reemerged from the nettles, he had been stung all over and the door was firmly closed. He straightened his tie and smoothed his thinning gray hair. Then, seeing no other alternative, he bent down and pushed open the flap of the letter box.

"That package is very old, so be careful with it," he shouted through the opening. "It's not meant for you. It's for someone called Archie Greene."

The letter box closed and then immediately opened again from the inside. "That's me!" cried the boy. "I'm Archie Greene!"

CHAPTER 3

An Honest Mistake

Archie sat in his small sitting room and stared at the package. Until that moment, he had been dreading the long and very lonely summer that lay ahead. His birthday always coincided with the start of the school holidays, and that usually meant six weeks of boredom. He had no brothers or sisters to play with, and the few friends he had at school would be going on expensive foreign holidays while he was stuck at home. But a mystery package—now that was exciting!

But his initial enthusiasm began to wane as he contemplated the strange-looking box. It looked old. It felt old. And, worst of all, it smelled old—of dust and cobwebs.

In Archie's experience, that probably meant it was old. Unfortunately, most of Archie's brief life so far had been spent trying to get away from old things.

He yearned for the smell of something new. Something bought from a proper shop. It wasn't that he was greedy or spoiled. In fact, it was the exact opposite. He had never owned anything brand-new.

The clothes he wore, the bed he slept in, and the plates he ate his food off were all old. Even the bicycle he'd gotten for Christmas last year was old. He loved it anyway. His gran had saved up all her money and bought it from an ad in the *West Wittering News*. She had made a great effort to do it up, but the chips to the red paint were unmistakable, and the gears clunked and rattled from a hard life.

Gran—her real name was Gardenia Greene—was the only thing in his life that Archie didn't mind being old. Her face was lined with the wear of seventy years, but her eyes still sparkled with life.

And it wasn't Gran's fault they had so little money. She hadn't asked to raise her grandson, after all. It had just happened that way. And even though Archie loved his gran very much, that didn't stop him from wondering what his life would be like if his parents had never left him with her as a baby to go on holiday with his older sister. If they'd never boarded that doomed ferryboat to France. Or if the captain hadn't dozed off at the wheel. Archie didn't really remember his mother and father. Nor did he remember his sister, who would have been nearly fifteen now, but it was always harder thinking about them on his birthday.

"Archibald!" His thoughts were interrupted by Gran calling from upstairs. "Who was that?"

"A man. He brought a parcel for me."

Gran's head appeared around the door. She had a pretty good idea what was in the package. She had spent the last twelve years dreading this moment. But now that it had arrived, she felt strangely relieved, as if a great weight had been lifted from her shoulders.

"Yes, I can see that," she said, trying to sound casual. "Do you know who it's from?"

Archie had no idea who had sent the package. He hesitated. Gran had brought him up to be cautious, but there was a part of him that longed for adventure. As he stared at the package, he could feel his curiosity stirring. He glanced at Gran.

She shrugged her bony shoulders. "Well, we can either sit here all night wondering what's inside that box or you can open it and find out. It's up to you."

Archie raised his eyebrows. He had never heard her speak like this before. He wondered if Gran knew more than she was letting on, but he didn't need any more encouragement.

He tugged at the twine, but the knots were so tightly tied that he could not loosen them. He held the parcel up to his mouth and tried to bite his way in. His lips brushed the parchment. It even tasted old—of dust and woodsmoke and something sweet, like honey, with a bitter tang. There was another flavor, too, something sharp and unpleasantly acidic, like vinegar. He wiped his lips, trying to get rid of the taste.

"Here, try these," Gran said, passing him the kitchen scissors.

Archie quickly cut through the twine. The parchment slackened and slithered to the floor. In his hand, he now held a wooden box stained with age. Archie eased it open, grinning.

~

As Horace Catchpole tramped back to the station, it started to rain. He felt utterly deflated—and now, to make matters worse, he was getting wet. He wiped his face with his now soggy handkerchief. When he had imagined what might be in the package, it had never occurred to him that it might be a boy's birthday present—and such a young boy, too. To think that it had been waiting in the firm's cellar all those years. Horace shook his head.

It was only when he was on the train back to London that Horace found the scroll. It was still in his pocket, where he had put it for safekeeping. In all the confusion, he had forgotten to deliver it with the package. This was a disaster! He had made a mistake, and a mistake of epic proportions!

As well as minding its own business, Folly & Catchpole's reputation was based on not making mistakes. Prudence Folly, the firm's senior partner, would be furious with him if she found out. But what could he do about it now?

The train he had boarded was an express train, and it didn't stop until it reached the outskirts of London over an hour and a half away. It would take him the same time again to get back to West Wittering—even if there was another train straightaway. He couldn't wait that long. What if the boy opened the package without knowing what the message said?

Sitting and fretting on the train, Horace had no way of knowing how serious his error was, or how costly it might prove, but he knew he had to make amends and had better do so immediately.

He looked at the scroll in his hands and weighed up his options. It was strictly against Folly & Catchpole's policy to open clients' packages or read their letters unless specifically instructed to do so. But Horace decided to take matters into his own hands. If the message was urgent, then he would have to turn around and go straight back. A lesser firm might try to contact the boy on the telephone, but Folly & Catchpole valued secrecy above all and only delivered messages in person. Horace took a deep breath and slipped the scroll from its ribbon.

CHAPTER 4

The Mysterious Symbol

It was beginning to get dark outside number three, Crabgate Cottages. Under the lamplight, Archie stared at the contents of the open wooden box in his lap. His nose was immediately overcome with a tickling sensation that exploded into a sneeze. Dust. The box was full of a talcum-powder-fine layer of white dust.

When the particles cleared, Archie peered inside. The box did not contain any great treasure—no jewel-encrusted dagger or gold coins or anything else exciting or dangerous.

"What is it, Archie?" Gran asked. She was still standing in the kitchen doorway.

"It's a book," he mumbled. "An old book."

"I thought it might be," she said with a resigned look on her face. "Who did you say delivered it?"

"Some law firm or other."

Gran's expression turned more anxious. "What law firm?"

"I don't know," Archie replied, distracted. "Just some law firm in London."

Gran's voice was sharp, which meant she was worried. "What was the firm called?"

"Oh, er, yeah. He said it was the oldest law firm in England. That's right. Two names. Very old-fashioned." Archie tried to recall his conversation on the doorstep. "Something and Catchpole."

"Folly! Folly and Catchpole."

"Yes, that sounds right." Archie nodded. "Why, do you know who it's from?"

Gran looked thoughtful. "No," she said. "I thought I might, but I don't. I was half expecting a book, but not this one. If it came from Folly and Catchpole, it could be very important and very serious. Did this man give you anything else? Like a . . . letter, for example?"

Archie shook his head. "Just the package."

"Hmm," Gran muttered. "That's strange. Oh well,

I'm sure it will all make sense later. And of course, you've always loved books."

It was true; Archie had always loved books. His gran said it was in his blood. But he had never seen a book quite like this one before. There was something very mysterious about it. It was as if it came from another time and place.

"What sort of book is it?" Gran asked.

Archie looked at the book's cover and realized that he couldn't read the title. He rubbed his eyes and looked again. The letters seemed vaguely familiar, but every time he tried to put them together to make words, they became indistinct and blurred. It was almost as if they were moving—going in and out of focus so he could never quite see them clearly. *It must be the dust in my eyes,* he thought. He squeezed his eyes closed and shook his head to clear it.

When he looked again, the letters appeared bright and clear for a moment, but just as Archie began to decipher them, they faded once more into the background of the dark cover. He turned his head to read the book's spine, but it was blank.

The odd thing was that Archie had the feeling that the writing was somehow familiar, in a peculiar, just-out-of-reach way, like something he knew but couldn't quite recall.

He reached forward and touched the book for the first time. As his fingers grazed the cover, a sharp pain shot up his arm. He pulled back his hand in surprise.

"Ouch!"

"What is it?" Gran asked.

"Dunno," Archie said, staring at his hand. "It felt like an electric shock."

Tentatively, he reached for the book again and wrapped his hand around the spine. Thankfully, this time there was no shock, and he lifted it free from its wooden box. The book was surprisingly light and bound in a dark leather cover that was stained with age. In one corner it had been scorched with fire, as if someone had tried to burn it and then thought better of it. This would explain the smell of woodsmoke.

Archie tried to open the book. But its cover was locked with a silver clasp etched with a strange symbol. Archie thought it resembled a matchstick person wearing a crescent moon crown with talons for feet.

He dug his fingernails under the silver clasp and pulled with all his might, but the clasp was securely fastened. He peered at the lock. When he turned a dial, different icons appeared in a small window. It reminded Archie of the mechanism on an old-fashioned safe. The trouble was he didn't know the right combination. He turned the dial clockwise until it made a loud click. A picture of a tree with a bolt of lightning appeared in the window, but the clasp was still shut tight. He turned it until it clicked again. This time a smiling skull appeared in the window, but the clasp would not budge.

Archie turned the clasp once more, and a crystal ball appeared. "Come on, open," he muttered under his breath.

With a dry click like snapping bone, the clasp sprang open. As it did, Archie caught a whiff of something sweet, like vanilla, and he thought he heard something. It sounded like an intake of breath: the sort a swimmer might make on surfacing, having been underwater for a long time. If he hadn't known better, Archie might have thought it came from the book itself. He put his ear to the leather cover. Silence.

CHAPTER 5

A Special Instruction

Holding his breath, Horace Catchpole slowly unrolled the scroll, taking care not to tear it. The parchment was dry and brittle, and he knew that it was very delicate. As he unwound it, his eyes were fixed on the writing as it gradually came into view. Horace gave a start. It was written in the Alphabet of the Magi, a language used by magicians and alchemists. There were few people left who could decipher it. Certainly the boy would not have been able to, but fortunately for Archie Greene, Horace Catchpole could: Folly & Catchpole specialized in rare languages.

Horace was feeling better about his decision already.

His language skills may have been a bit rusty, but he was determined to right his wrong and give the boy the translation. Taking out the pen and notepad he kept in his breast pocket, Horace began to translate a message that had not been seen for centuries. By the time he had finished, it was very late.

———

Archie was just dozing off to sleep when he heard the commotion outside. It sounded as if someone had run into a dustbin in the dark at high speed—and that was because someone had. There was a howl of pain and a crash as the wheelie bin went over. Then a brief silence and a scraping sound as the bin was picked up again, followed by a loud knocking on the door.

By the time Archie had thrown on his dressing gown and raced downstairs, Gran was already at the front door, and framed in the doorway was a very out-of-breath Horace Catchpole.

"That's him!" Archie cried. "That's the man who delivered the package!"

"Yes . . . yes . . . ," wheezed Horace, bent double to catch his breath. "I have to . . . tell you . . . something . . . I have a message . . . ," he panted.

Gran looked from the man to her grandson.

"I thought there was something missing," she said. "You'd better come in and explain what's going on."

At that moment, the grandfather clock in the corner struck midnight.

"Oh dear, oh dear," muttered Horace. "I just hope it's not too late."

"Too late for what?" asked Gran.

"When I delivered that parcel, I was supposed to give you a message that went with it. The instruction was very clear."

"This is exactly what I was worried about," sighed Gran. "Some packages have special conditions attached to them."

"That's right," said Horace.

"And this package is one of them," Gran continued.

"Ye-es. And, well," Horace said, "the thing is, the message with this package is written in a very old language, and it took me a while to translate. . . ."

"Really?" asked Archie, suddenly very interested. "What does it say?"

"It says that you have to take the contents of the package to the Aisle of White. Immediately."

"The Isle of Wight?" Archie asked hopefully. "Gran and I went there on holiday once."

"Er . . . no, not that Isle of Wight. This Aisle of White is a bookshop in Oxford," Horace interjected.

"Oxford!" Gran muttered. "I might have known."

"Might have known what?" Archie asked. Gran definitely knew more than she was letting on.

Gran tutted. "Well, I suppose you'll find out sooner or later. The Foxes live in Oxford—your aunt Loretta and her brood."

This was news to Archie. He wasn't aware that he had any relatives except Gran.

"The Foxes?" he said.

Gran's face creased. "Yes, Loretta and Woodbine Foxe. Sorry, I should have told you before, but it's been difficult. Loretta is your dad's sister."

Archie looked shocked. "So, you mean she's—"

"Yes." Gran nodded. "She's my daughter." She shook her head sadly. "It's a long story. . . . But if you're going to Oxford, then you should meet them." She paused and looked at Horace. "I suppose he will have to go to Oxford?"

Horace nodded. "Yes," he said. "You see, it's a Special Instruction, so there's no getting out of it. It means that whatever was in the package has to be brought on a given day. . . ."

"I thought so," said Gran, shaking her head. "And in this case, it is when?"

Horace gulped. "Er . . . that's the problem, you see. This Special Instruction was for today."

Horace glanced guiltily at the clock, which now said just after midnight. "Or rather, it was for yesterday," he added apologetically.

Archie took a moment to let Horace's words sink in. "So you mean we've missed it by a day?" he asked. "Does it matter?"

"It might matter a lot," Gran said gravely.

Horace looked at the two worried faces in front of him. "There's just one other thing," he said. "You didn't open it, did you . . . ?"

CHAPTER 6

The Aisle of White

Archie caught a bus to Oxford to find the Aisle of White. Gran had packed him off early that morning with a flask of tea and a bacon sandwich. She'd also given him a bag of clothes and suggested he might want to stay with his newfound cousins. Archie had been surprised that his usually cautious grandmother was sending him off on his own, but she had just told him that she "couldn't wrap him up in cotton wool forever."

"And besides," she'd added, planting a peck on his cheek, "there's something I need to take care of, and it will be easier without you under my feet. Now off you go . . . and remember your manners."

Gran seemed to know the Aisle of White bookshop well and had given him directions, along with the Foxes' address and a letter of introduction for his aunt. She'd also told him a bit about his cousins—unusual names, she said. They sounded like something from the woods—Hedge and Ditch or something like that. Archie had wanted to ask more questions, but there hadn't been time.

It was just after noon when Archie arrived. Compared to West Wittering, Oxford felt big and full of importance. There were lots of people on bicycles whizzing around in a hurry. He walked down the high street and turned left into a large cobbled square. His directions said the Aisle of White was across the square and down some narrow lanes.

He found the old bookshop in a small courtyard, wedged between a shop selling crystals and one that rented out fancy dress costumes. It was much smaller and shabbier than either of its two neighbors.

Above the green front door, in faded white-and-gold paint, a sign read THE AISLE OF WHITE: PURVEYOR OF RARE BOOKS. PROPRIETOR: GEOFFREY SCREECH. Archie felt a tingle of excitement. This was definitely the place! Another sign in the shop window, written in a spidery hand, declared WE BUY RARE BOOKS. INQUIRE WITHIN.

Encouraged, Archie pushed on the green door. As it opened, an old-fashioned bell clanged loudly, announcing his arrival. He felt like he was stepping back in time. The shop was bigger on the inside than it appeared on the outside, but it was by no means large. Dark wooden bookcases stood in columns, dividing the shop into a series of passages.

Archie couldn't imagine many people being interested in old books, so he was surprised to find three other customers lining up in front of him—a man, a woman, and a girl about his own age.

The salesperson facing them from behind a counter was a short, rather plump woman, deep in conversation with the man at the front of the line. The salesperson regarded the man, who was tall and stooped, through a pair of spectacles with lenses as thick as beer bottles. They seemed to be having a disagreement.

The woman in the line was fussing around the girl at her side, and Archie thought from the way they were behaving that they must be mother and daughter. Not having a mother of his own, Archie tended to notice such things. The mother was tall, with jet-black hair underneath a wide brimmed hat. The girl wore an expensive-looking green waxed-cotton coat that came to her knees, and her hair was pulled back into a severe ponytail. In her hands, she was holding an old book with a cover almost as battered as Archie's own.

No one noticed Archie, because the stooping man and the salesperson had started to argue loudly.

"Don't tell me you haven't seen it," the man said. "I tell you it's here somewhere! We've been waiting a long time for that book."

"Well, Dr. Rusp, I can only repeat what I have told you already," said the salesperson apologetically. "I have no idea what book you are referring to. I will talk to Geoffrey—Mr. Screech, that is—when he returns and see what he says, but I can assure you that no books arrived yesterday."

Archie gripped his book and wondered if it was the one the stooping man was expecting. He was on the point of saying something, when Dr. Rusp spoke again.

"I will have words with Screech about this!" he growled. "Where is the wretched man?"

"He—is—er—temporarily unavailable," the salesperson stammered.

"Pah!" spat Rusp. "He better have a good explanation for this outrage, or he will be permanently unavailable!"

As Dr. Rusp turned abruptly and swept out of the

shop, Archie hid his book behind his back. He didn't want
to hand it over to this bad-tempered man. He noticed that
the salesperson's hands were shaking, although she tried
to regain some composure by pushing her curly hair back
into the confines of its bun and attempting a smile at the
mother and daughter waiting for her attention.

"Good afternoon," she said.

"We have come to see Screech," the other woman said
forcefully. "He is expecting us." The girl didn't look in
the least bit interested and turned sulkily away from the
counter, looking at Archie suspiciously as she did so.

"As I just explained to Dr. Rusp, Mr. Screech is not
here at the moment," the salesperson said. "Can I help?"

"And who might you be?" the girl's mother asked
with no effort to disguise her irritation.

The woman behind the counter made another attempt
at a smile, but it was less convincing than the last one. "I
am Marjorie Gudge, senior assistant to Mr. Screech," she
declared. "I am in charge in his absence."

The girl's mother frowned. "Well, this is most unsatisfactory. We were told that Screech would be here in
person to meet us. We came yesterday, but the shop was
closed. It is a very important matter. I am Veronica Ripley,
and this is my daughter, Arabella."

Marjorie Gudge blinked nervously. "Oh, yes, of course, I know who you are, Mrs. Ripley. May I say what an honor it is to meet you and your charming daughter," she simpered. "It's so rare that I work in the front of the shop."

"Yes, yes," said Veronica Ripley dismissively. "We've brought the book!"

Marjorie Gudge looked mystified.

"The b-o-o-k," Veronica said, spelling out the letters for effect and nudging her daughter forward.

Arabella placed her book on the counter and gave a bored sigh. Marjorie Gudge picked it up and peered at it. "Gracious me," she said. "I wonder if that's the book Dr. Rusp was asking about."

"Certainly not!" Veronica raised her voice. "It is for Screech. It's a Special Instruction."

Marjorie regarded her over the rims of her glasses. "I don't know anything about that. Mr. Screech keeps a log of all his appointments. Perhaps it's in there on another day?"

She opened a leather-bound book on the counter and thumbed through the pages.

"Ah, here is this week's entry." Marjorie held the book up to her face. "Yes, you are correct. There's her name, 'Arabella Ripley,' right on yesterday's date." She turned the book around so the girl and her mother could see. "And there's a star next to it. Good for you!"

"But what does that little scribble in the margin say?" Veronica Ripley asked. "Maybe it was your meeting time, darling. Arabella, can you see?"

Arabella peered at the page again. "It's all crossed out," she whined. "But it looks like it says 'Archie Greene.'"

Archie looked up sharply at the sound of his name.

"Well," said Marjorie, shaking her head, "I do apologize. I will ask Mr. Screech to contact you on his return, but I will have to take this book for safekeeping. It is a Special Instruction, after all."

"This is most unsatisfactory!" Veronica Ripley declared. "Have Screech call us the moment he returns. Come on, Arabella." She sniffed. "We know where we're not appreciated!"

The Ripleys stormed out, with Arabella giving Archie an evil look as she barged past.

Marjorie Gudge picked up the book on the counter and examined it. "It's an almanac from 1603," she said to herself. "Well, I never."

Archie's ears pricked up. He wondered if his book was as old as the almanac.

"Hello," he said, offering a smile and holding up his

book. "I was told to bring this here."

Marjorie Gudge paid him no attention. The Aisle of White's senior assistant was far more concerned with the book in her hands.

Archie cast his eyes around the bookshop. It really was odd. The shop was lit by flickering candlelight—very atmospheric but not very helpful for reading. How anyone could possibly find what they were looking for was a mystery to Archie. There were no signs either, so he couldn't tell where nonfiction stopped and fiction began. The shelves that formed the aisles were packed with books of all shapes and sizes, but unlike most modern books, which were designed to grab the browser's attention, these looked like they wanted to be anonymous. Their spines all seemed the same. The titles and the names of their authors were faded.

The shop had the same aroma as his book— woodsmoke, cobwebs, and candle wax. Leaving Marjorie to the almanac, he was wandering down an aisle when he thought he heard something.

It sounded like voices whispering, and it seemed to be coming from behind a black velvet curtain to one side of the counter. Archie leaned in closer. There it was again!

Archie peered behind the curtain. "Hello?" he said.

"Is there someone there?"

"What's that, dear?" Marjorie Gudge said, noticing him for the first time.

"I thought I heard something," he mumbled. "Never mind."

"Right then, what can I do for you?"

"Er, I was told to bring this book here," Archie said, proudly producing his book.

"Put it there with the other new arrivals," she said, indicating a cardboard box on the counter.

She slid the ledger across the counter. "Write down your details, and Mr. Screech will be in touch. Now I'd better get these down to the workshop," she added, picking up a pile of books.

Archie reluctantly put his book in the box just as Marjorie Gudge dropped what she'd just picked up.

"Let me help you," said Archie, bending down.

"They've got to go downstairs to be mended," Marjorie said.

"I can carry them if you want," Archie offered.

"That's very kind, dear," she replied. "It's nice to meet a kind customer, for a change." She tugged the velvet curtain to one side and bustled through the opening.

"This way," she called over her shoulder.

Archie scooped up as many of the tatty books as he could carry and followed Marjorie down a dark passage, lit by flickering candlelight. Her ringlets cast bobbing shadows on the wall.

When they reached the end of the passage, Marjorie took a lantern from a shelf and balanced it on top of the pile of books in his arms.

"Careful," she cautioned, pointing to a long spiral staircase leading downward. "It's a bit steep."

"Thanks," Archie said, peering around the lantern and down the stairs.

"Take the books to Old Zeb—third door on the right," she said, giving him a meaningful look. "Remember that, it's important. You don't want to be getting lost down there."

"Third door on the right," Archie repeated. "Old Zeb. Got it."

At the bottom of the stairs, Archie found himself in another long and even dimmer corridor. The air smelled earthy and damp, and by the light of his lantern, he could see three tall, arched, Gothic-style doors like the ones he'd expect to find in a castle. Each door was a different color. The first door was green. The second door was blue. The third door was red. Outside each door, a flaming torch was set in an iron bracket mounted on the wall, giving off the pungent aroma of burning asphalt.

Archie was beginning to have second thoughts. He felt butterflies in his stomach and his mouth was dry, but his curiosity was increasing with every step. He wondered where Marjorie Gudge was sending him.

"The third door," he said to himself under his breath. He began to count as he passed them. "One, two . . ." He was about to move down the corridor when he thought he heard a deep cracking noise, like ice breaking on a frozen lake. It seemed to be coming from behind the blue door. The air coming from under the door felt like an arctic chill, but when he put his ear to it, there was only silence.

Archie quickly walked on. The third door was slightly ajar. Archie eased it open with his elbow. "Uh . . . Old Zeb?" he called.

"Yeeees?" said a wheezy, high-pitched voice.

CHAPTER 7

Old Zeb

A rchie stepped into a large workshop. The room smelled strongly of old parchment. Strewn all over the flagstone floor were offcuts of leather and bits of twine. Metal tools hung haphazardly on the walls. Archie, though, was drawn to the large wooden workbench running down the center of the workshop, cluttered with piles of books like the ones he had brought from the shop.

"Better put those down," the voice said. "Don't want to damage them any more by dropping them."

Archie gratefully set down the books on the end of the bench. His arms felt stiff from carrying them. He looked around him to locate the source of the voice.

"Hello?" he called.

"I'm over here," the voice wheezed. "By the smithy."

Standing beside a furnace at one end of the room was a tiny old man, no more than four feet tall. He had scraggy white hair that stood up almost vertically in tufts on an otherwise bald head, and a thin red face with two bright-green eyes above a hooked nose. The little man was wearing some sort of coverall that covered his legs and torso but left his arms completely bare.

The man's thin, white, muscly arms looked like knotted pieces of string. The little man gestured at the room.

"Welcome to the Mending Workshop," he said. "I am Mr. Perret, the bookbinder, but most people call me Old Zeb."

He licked his lips, reminding Archie of a reptile. Not a snake but a small lizard—a gecko, perhaps.

"And what is your name, young man?"

"Me? Oh, I'm Archie," Archie said in a faltering voice.

Old Zeb looked him up and down. Then he scratched the end of his long nose.

"Well, pleased to meet you, Archie."

He gave a chuckle, and his eyes glinted with a mad look. Then he scratched his nose again, and his expression turned serious.

"But first things first. You can't judge a book by its cover. Have to find out if it's got a good spine!"

The old man was talking in riddles, but Archie smiled politely, humoring him. Old Zeb continued. "It's all about passing on the flame, you see. The question is: are you someone I could pass the flame to? Show me your hands!"

Archie held out his hands. The bookbinder held them by the wrists. The old man's own hands were surprisingly powerful.

"Hmm," he muttered to himself. "Good hands, these." He turned them over to inspect the palms. "Honest hands," he added. "But are they strong enough? Need strong hands to be a bookbinder. Need quick hands, too."

Old Zeb licked his lips thoughtfully. "Let's see what the old Word Smithy says!"

Releasing Archie's wrists, he slipped on a thick leather glove and opened the door to the furnace. The fire made a hissing sound and gave off a plume of white smoke.

"The Word Smithy knows," he continued. "Its flame has been burning for thousands of years."

The old man suddenly pulled a yellow flame from the furnace, and to Archie's horror, he hurled it toward a pile of books on the workbench. Archie instinctively shot out a hand and caught the flame.

In that split second he realized what a foolish thing he'd done. He flinched, expecting the flame to burn his skin, but he felt nothing except a warm, tingling sensation on his palm.

Archie stared at the flame still burning on his hand—twisting and writhing into different shapes. He was quite unable to drag his eyes away from it.

"It's beautiful," he mumbled. "But why isn't it burning me?"

"Pharos—the Flame of Alexandria—the light of the world!" breathed Old Zeb. "It won't burn you."

Archie couldn't believe his eyes. He was only supposed to be dropping off books, but now he was catching fire!

The flame changed from yellow to blue and then vanished. The palm of Archie's right hand immediately began to itch. He was sure it must have been burned after all, but when he looked, there was just a tiny red mark like a small tattoo.

He was suddenly aware of Old Zeb's sparkling eyes. "Show me your hand again," the old man said. "The one that held the flame."

Archie held out his hand. The bookbinder seized it and turned it over so that the palm faced him.

"Excellent," he muttered, a big smile spreading across his face.

He took something from his pocket and dabbed at Archie's hand. It felt wet and stung slightly. "There," he said kindly. "That'll soothe the itching. You won't feel a thing in a couple of days."

Archie stared at the tiny red mark on his hand. "How weird," he said. "It didn't hurt at all."

The old man nodded. "Yes, it's called a Firemark. There's one for each of the three book skills—Finding, Binding, and Minding." Archie didn't know what to make of what Old Zeb was telling him, but the book-binder interrupted his thoughts.

"Now then," he said, "let's get down to business. We start at nine sharp and we work until the work is done— or I've had enough. Mostly you will be mending books, but sometimes you will have to deliver them back to where they belong. Don't worry, I'll tell you more about that later. We'll get you started tomorrow. Now, I'm for-getting my manners. Come along, come along, let's have some tea."

Was this funny little man offering him a job? Archie wondered. It certainly sounded like it. It all seemed a bit quick, but perhaps that was how they did things in Oxford. Archie could think of worse things than working in a bookshop. But what would Gran say? She didn't like him talking to strangers—and Old Zeb was certainly strange.

The old bookbinder poured two cups from an old, cracked brown teapot and licked his lips again. He definitely reminded Archie of a gecko.

"Now, what's your surname?"

"Greene," Archie replied, still looking at his hand.

"Oh!" the old man exclaimed excitedly. "Greene, is it? You'd be one of those Greenes then, would you?"

The old bookbinder thought for a moment. "So, you must be Alex's son?"

Archie started at the sound of his father's name. "Yes, but how did you know?"

The old man gave a chuckle. "I could tell you a few things about the Greenes, I could!" He picked up a set of bellows almost as big as he was and pumped some air into the furnace, smiling as it roared into life.

"A Greene," the old man declared, holding up his teacup to make a toast.

"Who would have thought?" Old Zeb winked. "I taught your dad, of course."

Archie forgot all about the Firemark and the job offer. Old Zeb had taught his father! Gran had told him that Alex Greene had taught geography in a local school. Archie suddenly realized how little he knew about his family. He hadn't even known he had cousins. He wondered again why Gran hadn't mentioned them before and felt a tingle of anticipation that he'd be meeting them that very afternoon.

Archie held up his own teacup, and the little man chinked his cup against it.

"Cheers!" Old Zeb cried. "Welcome on board, Archie Greene! See you tomorrow."

CHAPTER 8

Houndstooth Road

Archie left the Aisle of White with his head in a spin. A lot of strange things had happened in the last few hours, and he seemed to be at the center of them all. Outside, it was starting to cloud over, but at least it wasn't raining. At that moment, a solitary ray of sunlight found its way into the courtyard outside the bookshop and glinted off the shop sign like a smile.

Archie followed the directions to his cousins' house. Gran had said it was walking distance from the center of Oxford, and sure enough, half an hour later, he arrived at 32 Houndstooth Road. It wasn't hard to spot—it was the only purple house on the street. He pressed the doorbell.

Archie's heart was beating fast. He hadn't realized quite how nervous, as well as excited, he was about meeting his relatives. What if they didn't know who he was? Or what if they didn't like him? He glanced anxiously at the door.

Nothing happened. He waited what he considered to be a reasonable amount of time—what Gran would call a polite amount of time—and then he rang again. Still nothing. What if no one was at home? Where would he stay? Perhaps this wasn't the right address after all. Or maybe the Foxes had moved. He took a deep breath and gave a sharp knock on the door. He heard footsteps. Then the door shuddered open just enough for someone to peer out. Two dark eyes regarded Archie from inside the house.

"No thanks, we don't want any," the owner of the dark eyes said in an impudent voice. "And if you're after money, forget it, we haven't got any. Actually, we don't even live here anymore."

Archie looked into the dark eyes. They belonged to a boy a little younger than him, with brown, tousled hair and freckles.

"Excuse me," Archie said, in his politest voice, "I am looking for the Foxe family."

The boy looked shifty. He glanced over his shoulder. Archie got the impression that there was someone else lurking behind the door, telling the boy what to say.

"I'm a relative," Archie added. "Granny Greene sent me."

There was rustling of clothes as someone who had been crouching down stood up. Then the door flew open, and Loretta Foxe appeared next to the boy. She beamed at Archie.

"Granny Greene sent you?" she cried.

Archie nodded and took a step back in alarm. "Yes," he answered cautiously.

Loretta suddenly threw her arms around him and hugged him. "My dear boy, how wonderful to see you!"

Archie gazed as she danced a little celebratory jig on the doorstep.

"Don't worry about Mum," the dark-haired boy said. "She's a bit mental, but you get used to her after a while. I'm Thistle, by the way." He extended his hand to Archie and grinned.

"I'm Archie," he replied, shaking the boy's hand.

"And I am Loretta," the woman announced, smiling. "Aunt Loretta to you!"

Archie was aware that she was staring at him in a most peculiar way. He felt suddenly shy.

"Well, well, well," she said, shaking her head as if she couldn't quite believe what she was seeing. "You're the absolute spit of your father when he was your age. I've got some photos of him I'll show you later. Come in! Come in!"

Loretta swept Archie and Thistle along a short hallway and into the kitchen.

The first thing Archie noticed about the Foxe residence was that there was a preponderance of purple. The walls and woodwork were all painted in different shades of it. The second thing that occurred to him was that there were an awful lot of books. The walls were completely lined with bookcases from floor to ceiling. In fact, everywhere Archie looked there were even more books. He had to step over stacks of them on the floor, and every surface in the house seemed to have more books piled on it.

"Sit down, sit down," said Loretta. "Make yourself at home."

Archie pulled out a chair and sat, being careful not to bump a tower of books balanced on the kitchen table. Thistle pulled out the chair opposite.

"Are you thirsty, dear?" Loretta leaned over Archie's shoulder. "Would you like a drink? We've got some very nice elderberry squash."

"No, I'm fine," Archie said, feeling self-conscious. "Thank you."

"I'm thirsty, Mum," Thistle said. "Can I have a drink?"

"Yes, of course, my dear. Now be a good boy and get it yourself. Water, mind—those elderberries don't grow on trees."

Archie noticed that Thistle helped himself to a drink of elderberry squash anyway.

"And how is Mum . . . I mean Granny Greene?" asked Loretta.

"She's very well," Archie replied politely. "She sent you a letter," he added, pulling it from his pocket and handing it to her.

Loretta took a big breath and opened the envelope. She flapped the folded letter open and read it to herself.

My Dear Loretta,

I am writing to introduce Archie—your nephew. I think it would be best if he stays with you for a time—a few weeks at least.

Until yesterday the promise I made to your brother tied my hands. But someone has sent Archie a book for his twelfth birthday—and it has come with a Special Instruction.

I am sure I don't need to tell you how concerning this is. I had hoped Archie's life would take another course. I can't pretend otherwise. But I fear that he cannot avoid his destiny.

There are some matters that I must attend to urgently, and it will be easier if I know that the boy is safe.

Please take good care of Archie and help him find his way. He is a good boy and dearer to me than breath.

Please give my love to the children and to Woodbine.

Fondest regards,
Your mother

Loretta slipped the letter into a drawer. She was delighted to see her long-lost nephew, but the tone of the letter worried her. What was this mysterious book? She didn't want to alarm Archie, but she was intrigued and more than a little anxious.

To calm her mind, she began to fuss about the

kitchen, opening and closing cupboards and drawers, taking out and then putting away a selection of crockery and cutlery.

There was one cupboard door that Loretta did not open. It was in the middle of the wall. Archie wondered what was in it. At that moment, the cupboard flew open and a face appeared. Two gray crinkly eyes looked into the room. Archie, who was not used to seeing heads appear in cupboards, stared. The face was framed by straw-like hair that reminded Archie of a scarecrow.

"What ho!" said the scarecrow. "What's all the noise about?"

Archie could see now that it wasn't a cupboard; it was a serving hatch connecting the kitchen to the room next door.

"There you are, Woodbine," said Loretta. "We have a guest."

The gray crinkly eyes swiveled to look.

"Archie, this is your uncle Woodbine."

"What ho, young'un!" Woodbine's lined face broke into a wide crooked smile. He reached through the hatch, and they shook hands. Woodbine's grip was so tight that Archie thought it might crush his fingers.

"Pleased to meet you," Archie said politely. His strange

day had just gotten stranger.

Woodbine nodded sagely, and Thistle grinned, and even though he'd only just met them, Archie felt comfortable among these strange people. There was something familiar and oddly reassuring about them. Something that felt like home—so much so that when Loretta said, "Of course, you will stay for the summer?" Archie found himself nodding his head enthusiastically.

Thistle broke into a broad smile. "Excellent! I can't wait to tell Bram!"

"Bram?" asked Archie.

"Yeah," Thistle replied. "My sister—Bramble. She's not my real sister, though. Can't be, she's too ugly!"

"Thistle!" his mother said, catching hold of his ear. "Of course Bramble is your real sister, and she should be home by now. I wonder what's keeping her."

"Ouch!" Thistle said. "Let go!"

"Now, then," said Loretta, releasing her son. "You can all help me make the sandwiches. Except Archie. He's our guest."

She disappeared into the walk-in larder and returned carrying a half-eaten birthday cake with blue icing, which she placed on the table.

She nodded to herself in a self-satisfied way and

flashed a smile. "There," she said. "I made a cake for your birthday, Archie."

"A birthday cake for me?" asked Archie, with a note of surprise. "But how did you know I was coming?"

Loretta smiled. "I had a feeling you might drop by," she said. "What with it being your twelfth birthday and all."

CHAPTER 9

Foxe Sandwiches for Tea

A few minutes later, Bramble Foxe strode into the kitchen carrying a large cardboard box.

"What ho!" she called, in a loud, cheerful voice like Woodbine's.

"Ah, there you are, Bramble," Loretta said. "This is your cousin Archie. And Archie, this is your cousin Bramble."

"Cousin?" said Bramble. "Since when did we have a cousin?"

Loretta gave her a dark look. "You've always had a cousin, you just hadn't met him before. Now say hello."

Bramble grinned. "All right, Archie?"

Archie smiled awkwardly. Bramble seemed a bit older than him.

"He's my brother's son," said Loretta in reply to Bramble's unspoken question. "He's going to be staying with us for a while. Anyway, where've you been all this time, darling? I was starting to worry."

"We were late getting out," Bramble said. "There's something odd going on at work. Apparently a boy was attacked. I've got a note about a special meeting later this week. No one knows what it's about, but we've all been told to be extra vigilant."

She put the cardboard box on the kitchen floor. Archie peered across the table and saw that the box was full of old books. Bramble pulled out a chair.

"Looks like a good haul," Woodbine said, rubbing his hands together.

"Yes," said Bramble. "I picked them up from a thrift shop on the way home. But I'm not sure any of them are keepers."

"All right, enough shoptalk at teatime," Loretta said. "Would you like a sandwich, dear?" she asked Archie, holding out a plate. Archie, who had watched her prepare them with growing apprehension, did his best to look hungry.

"Yes, please," he said.

"These are lemon curd and ketchup. These are tuna and jam, and these are cheese . . . and banana." Loretta pointed a purple fingernail at each one.

Archie's hand hesitated in midair. He caught sight of Thistle and Bramble both watching to see how he would react. He knew his credibility was on the line.

"I'll try the banana and cheese," he said, helping himself from the plate and taking a big bite. His cousins grinned.

"Tuck in, everyone!" Loretta trilled.

This appeared to be a signal for Thistle, Bramble, and Woodbine to wage war with one another. They immediately began grabbing the sandwiches within reach and piling them onto their plates. Then they feverishly opened the little unlabeled jars of homemade this and that, sniffed them, and, thrusting their knives, forks, and spoons inside, extracted the contents. All of this activity was combined with elbow jousting to fend off anyone else who might be going for the same morsel of food.

Archie found it all highly entertaining. One minute, he was sitting with four human beings; the next, three of them had embarked on a food frenzy that would have shamed a troupe of baboons.

"Now, Thistle, remember your manners!" cried Loretta, swatting Thistle's hand with a dish towel as he reached across Archie to pour himself a drink. "Really, Woodbine, do you have to eat three sandwiches at once? Don't forget our guest, Bramble—make sure you leave some for Archie."

Archie made a grab for a sandwich, just beating Thistle to it. Thistle roared with mock indignation and grabbed some chips from under Bramble's nose. Bramble, meanwhile, was cutting a piece of birthday cake with one hand while pouring some elderberry squash with the other. Archie was impressed.

"How do you do that?" he asked, admiring her ambidexterity.

Bramble grinned. "Years of practice!" she said. "Would you like some of *your* birthday cake before Thistle scarfs the lot?"

Archie helped himself to a large slice, cramming it into his mouth like his cousins. The sardine filling was unexpected, but it went surprisingly well with the chocolate sponge and blueberry icing. He wondered again why Loretta had made him a birthday cake. How had she known that he would be coming to Oxford? Perhaps the book was from her?

"So, Archie, tell us about this book that Granny Greene mentioned in her letter," Loretta said.

Not from her, after all. Archie had the full attention of all four Foxes now. Even Woodbine stopped chewing and trained his crinkly eyes on him.

Archie explained about the visit from Horace Catchpole and the mix-up over the message, and how Horace had come back later that night. At the mention of a Special Instruction, the Foxes exchanged looks.

"So you were a day late?" Loretta asked thoughtfully.

"Yes," confirmed Archie. "Gran was a bit worried about that. Do you think it matters?"

"Well, it wasn't your fault it arrived late, dear. The important thing is that you followed the instruction as soon as you could," Loretta said, but Archie thought she gave Woodbine a worried glance. "What happened next?"

Archie told them about Veronica Ripley and Arabella, her sullen-faced daughter.

"And they brought a book like me, and Veronica said that was a Special Instruction, too," said Archie.

"Hmm," muttered Woodbine. "One Special Instruction is rare enough, but two on the same day—that is unusual. I would have expected Geoffrey Screech to have been there to receive them in person."

"Marjorie Gudge said he was supposed to be back yesterday," said Archie, "but he was delayed. Marjorie sent the Ripleys away. I think they were a bit annoyed. And then this funny little man called Old Zeb offered me some silly job."

"A job?" said Loretta sharply.

"Well, I took some books to his workshop for the salesperson, and he kept going on about it. I thought he might've been a bit crazy, to be honest."

The Foxes were watching him intently.

"Did you touch the flame?" Loretta asked urgently. "Show me!"

Archie held out his hand and she peered at his palm.

"You're Old Zeb's apprentice," she said, glancing at Woodbine. "There can be no mistake about it."

"How do you know?" asked Archie, staring at the tattoo-like mark, which he noticed resembled a tiny needle and thread.

"Because the flame is binding," said Woodbine. "Once you have the Firemark, you are bound to your apprenticeship. You'll have to show up tomorrow."

"Bramble has one like it," said Loretta. "Show Archie your hand."

Bramble held out her palm to reveal a blue mark, with

a symbol of a ladder. Next to it was another one in green with a symbol of an eye.

"Bramble is in her second year," Loretta explained. "She's a Second Hand—that's why she has her second Firemark. And Thistle here will start his apprenticeship next year when he turns twelve," Loretta continued. "That's the age that all the apprentices start."

Archie's brow furrowed. "I can understand why you like books," he said. "I like books, too. But do you really want to make your hobby your job?"

Loretta gave him another sharp look. "Hobby?" she cried. "It isn't a hobby, dear. And they're not just any old books. We're the Flame Keepers of Alexandria. We look after magical books."

CHAPTER 10

The Flame Keepers

Archie stared at his aunt. He must have misheard her.

"Did you just say you are the Flame Keepers of . . . ?"

"Alexandria," Loretta finished the sentence for him. "Yes."

Archie considered this for a moment. That was the second time in one day he'd heard about Alexandria. He shook his head to clear it. It must be a family joke, he thought. He looked at the others around the table. Woodbine and his two cousins looked back at him with no hint of a smile.

"And you said the books were . . . magic?" Archie

could hardly believe his ears.

"Yes dear. We save them," said Loretta.

Archie blinked. He felt that he had stumbled into some parallel universe. Here they were talking about magical books as if it was all perfectly normal. They couldn't be serious, surely? He thought back to catching the flame in the bookshop. Or could they?

"These magical books," he said. "How do you save them?"

"We return them to the Museum of Magical Miscellany, of course," said Bramble. "Didn't Old Zeb explain?"

"The Museum of what . . . ?" Archie spluttered.

Bramble looked at her mother incredulously. "How can he be related to us and not know about the museum?"

"Granny Greene thought it best not to tell him," Loretta said. "She had her reasons, but it is time now for Archie to learn about our world—his world."

She turned to Archie. "The Museum of Magical Miscellany is a closely guarded secret. It is hidden beneath the Bodleian Library in Oxford. But I think we'd better start at the beginning."

Dusk was falling outside, spilling darkness into the room where they sat. Woodbine took a box of matches from his pocket and lit two candlesticks on the kitchen table. The fire cast dancing shadows on the wall.

"Most people have forgotten about magic or don't know it ever existed, but there was a time when it flourished," Loretta explained, "a Golden Age of Magic. In those days the most powerful magicians in the world created spells, enchantments, and charms, which they wrote down in books for others to use. These are the same books that magicians have relied on ever since.

"When Alexander the Great built his empire, he collected magic from every country he conquered. He amassed all manner of magical instruments and artifacts. He even had his own magical gardens and a menagerie of magical creatures. But what Alexander prized above all else was his collection of magical books.

"It was the greatest collection of magical knowledge ever assembled and the most valuable as well. In Egypt, Alexander planned a great library to house his collection and keep it safe—the Great Library of Alexandria. He died before it was completed, but he gave the task of protecting the magical books to his most trusted scribes."

"In the harbor in Alexandria, on the island of Pharos, a great lighthouse was built to guide travelers to the library. The Flame of Pharos lit that lighthouse, and the library's guardians were responsible for ensuring that the Flame was never extinguished. It is the same Flame that burns in Old Zeb's smithy and left that mark on your hand."

The candles flickered, and Loretta fell silent. Woodbine took up the story.

"For centuries Alexander's collection was kept safe, until in 48 BC something terrible happened. A dark sorcerer called Barzak started a fire, and the Great Library was burned down. When the scribes tried to salvage what remained of Alexander's collection, they discovered that the magic books had been corrupted—tainted by Barzak's dark sorcery. Centuries later the damaged books were brought here to Oxford, where they would be safe."

Woodbine shook his head sadly. "The burning of the Great Library brought an end to the Golden Age of Magic. It marked the beginning of a Dark Age. Ordinary people grew suspicious of magic, frightened by it, and with good cause. Spells were cast out of spite and to cause mischief. Alchemists experimented wildly to make gold and become rich. Sorcerers summoned dark spirits. It was a bad time, and people who practiced magic were put on trial for witchcraft. Some wondered whether magic itself could survive."

"And then in the 1600s a promising English alchemist called Fabian Grey emerged, and the magical world believed that he might be the one to save magic. But Grey became intoxicated with his own power. In 1666, his reckless experiments started the Great Fire of London—the second great magical conflagration. And so the world's magicians met in London and agreed that such a disaster must never happen again. They formed the Magical League and introduced strict new Lores on the use of magic.

Woodbine's brow darkened. "But not everyone in the magical world agreed with the new Lores. In secret, there were some who still used magic for their own purposes. There still are. We call them Greaders—because they are greedy for the magic in the books."

A breeze blew into the room from an open window, making the flames from the candles bob and flicker. Woodbine dropped his voice to a whisper.

"Above all else, the Greaders desire a small number of very powerful magical books. The Terrible Tomes are the seven most dangerous dark magic books ever written. It is said that if the Greaders get their hands on just one of the Terrible Tomes, they could destroy the world."

Archie was silent for a moment. His mind was racing.

"So, is my book magical?" he asked.

"Almost certainly," said Loretta.

"I knew there was something special about that book," he said. "But why would someone send me a magical book?"

"I would have thought that was obvious," said Loretta.

Archie stared at her uncomprehendingly.

"You come from one of the families who looked after Alexander's original collection. We all do—the Foxes, the Ripleys, Marjorie Gudge—even old Rusp. Magic books are in our blood. We are responsible for preserving the magic that remains. If someone wanted to keep a book safe, they would send it to one of the Flame Keepers. That way they'd be sure it would be taken to the Aisle of White and returned to the museum."

Archie's mouth fell open. "I see," he managed to stammer. "Why didn't Gran tell me any of this before?"

Loretta gave him a kindly smile. "Your father made her promise to keep you away from magic for your own safety."

"And with good reason," said Bramble. "Dark magic can be dangerous. I told you a boy was attacked recently, didn't I? When the Greaders start coming to Oxford, you know there's going to be trouble."

CHAPTER 11

Quill's Chocolate House

When Archie woke the next morning, the first thing he saw was Thistle's grinning face.

"Come on, Sleeping Beauty—wakey, wakey! Mum says breakfast's on the table. Oh, and she asked me to give you this," he added, putting a shoe box down on the table next to Archie's bed.

"It's some of your dad's old things. Mum's been keeping them for you. But she says you'll have to look at them later. Bramble wants to show you around the museum before you start your first day as an apprentice. You'd better get a move on."

Archie stared at his younger cousin. It was true then—

he hadn't dreamed it. He put the shoe box under his bed, dressed, and raced down the stairs.

The sunshine radiated down onto the streets of Oxford. As Archie strolled along beside Bramble, he found himself whistling as he walked.

"The great thing about Oxford is that there's so much history," confided Bramble. "The museum's been here for centuries, and most people don't even know it exists."

Archie could see that Oxford, with its ancient buildings, gated courtyards, and winding cobbled streets, was made for secrets.

They turned left along a very wide road called Broad Street, and Archie noticed two grand buildings on the right. The first was some sort of theater, and the second was the Bodleian Library, where the Museum of Magical Miscellany was located. But to his surprise, Bramble marched straight past the entrance.

"Aren't we going in?" he asked.

She smiled. "You didn't think we would walk in the front door, did you? That'd be a bit obvious. There's a secret entrance that only the Flame Keepers know about."

Now that she explained it, it made sense. Of course

the Museum of Magical Miscellany would need a secret entrance. Bramble strode on, and Archie had to jog to catch her.

"Most of the world has forgotten that magic ever existed," Bramble continued. "They think it's just something from storybooks. It's a good thing, too, Mum says, because people today aren't ready for magic. That's why we call them the Unready. They don't know about the magic books, and it's better that it stays that way. They have enough trouble with money, Mum says."

As she spoke, Bramble turned right into a side street. Archie hurried after her. She was still talking.

"Dad says that the Unready have science instead of magic—it's easier and less tempting. Besides, if people knew about the magic books, it would cause all sorts of arguments. Imagine if one country had more magic than another—there'd be wars and all sorts of rows. Just like there used to be!"

They had reached the cobbled square Archie had seen the day before. Bramble marched purposefully across it and entered the narrow lanes.

When there was no one near, she stopped and faced him. "What you need to know, Archie, is that it's against the Lore to tell anyone about the magic books unless they belong to the Magical League. That's why Mothballs is such a secret."

"Mothballs?"

Bramble smiled mischievously. "Yes, that's what the apprentices call the museum."

Archie felt a thrill of excitement. All his life he had dreamed of adventure, and now he really was in the middle of one.

"Okay, I get it. So where is it, this secret entrance?"

"You'll see." Bramble grinned and set off again.

She suddenly ducked through an archway and into the courtyard that led to the Aisle of White.

"Is it through the bookshop?" Archie asked.

Bramble shook her head. "The Aisle of White is the only part of Mothballs that's open to the Unready—so they can bring in magical books if they find them. Not that they'd be able to tell if a book was magic. Mr. Screech figures that out. But the main museum is strictly for Flame Keepers."

She crossed to the other side of the enclosed courtyard, to an old and shabby half-timbered building with exposed beams in the medieval style. The spaces between the uneven timbers were filled with discolored plaster, and the upstairs bulged out beyond the ground floor. A sign outside declared it to be QUILL'S COFFEE & CHOCOLATE HOUSE, ESTABLISHED 1657. EXOTIC COFFEE AND CHOC-OLATE FROM AROUND THE WORLD, the sign promised. CHOC-TAILS SERVED. A steady stream of teenage boys and girls were coming and going.

"Ta-da!" she said, indicating the door to Quill's, which was down some stone steps.

Archie couldn't imagine a more unlikely way into a museum. He grinned. "Good disguise."

Bramble smiled. "Yes," she chuckled. "Isn't it? Now get a move on before people start wondering why we're standing here gabbing."

At the bottom of the steps, a heavy oak door led into Quill's. Bramble pushed it and they slipped inside. An auburn-haired girl a little younger than Bramble came in just behind them.

A delicious aroma of chocolate, suffused with coffee, vanilla, orange, and other fragrant flavors, wafted through the air. Archie noticed that unlike its gloomy exterior, on the inside Quill's was bathed in a warm, sunny light. A sunbeam blazed through a glass skylight and reflected off the polished wooden floor, lending Quill's a mystical, almost astral quality.

As Archie watched, the girl with auburn hair strolled

toward the light. It was so bright that Archie had to shield his eyes. When he looked again, she had vanished.

"That's odd," he said. "Where did that girl go?"

Bramble smiled in a knowing way. "You'll find out soon enough," she said.

Directly opposite them was a long wooden bar. Ranged along the bar in a row were twenty or more chrome taps with old-fashioned porcelain handles.

A waitress pulled down on one of the handles, and a torrent of molten chocolate gushed into the mug she was holding. Then she held a glass under another tap. This time a stream of a red fruit juice gushed out. Archie licked his lips.

He was suddenly aware of the waitress looking at him. She was tall and thin with bare arms and lots of tattoos. Her hair was short and spiky and very, very black. Both her eyebrows were pierced.

"That's Pink," Bramble said quietly. "She controls who goes in and out. Hello, Pink," she called. "This is my cousin Archie Greene."

Pink gave him a friendly nod and came over. "So you're Alex Greene's boy. I knew your dad."

Bramble lowered her voice to a conspiratorial whisper. "He's the new Bookbinding apprentice, and he's never seen the museum before."

Pink smiled good-naturedly. "Following in the family footsteps, then—good for you, Arch."

She leaned forward secretively. "I take it you've got the mark?"

"Yes, he has." Bramble nodded. "Show Pink your hand."

Archie revealed his magic mark.

Pink squinted at it. "Yep, that's all in order. You can pass through the Door Ray."

Bramble took him by the arm and marched him straight through the shaft of light. It felt warm like sunshine, and for a moment, Archie was dazzled by it. He smelled a strange aroma that put him in mind of a summer's night. Then he was on the other side.

CHAPTER 12

The Seats of Learning

Archie found himself in a large room that he hadn't noticed before. From this side it was obvious that Quill's had two distinct parts to it. At the front it looked like an ordinary café, but at the back there was a much larger space that was invisible from the other side. Separating the two was the shaft of light.

From where he was now, Archie could see into the front of the shop as if it were on the other side of a window. The effect was like a one-way mirror. He could see the people at the front of the shop but could not be seen by them.

"That's weird," he said to Bramble. "When you first

come in, you wouldn't know this side was here at all."

"Exactly." Bramble smiled. "Anyone can walk in off the street, but only the Flame Keepers can pass through the Door Ray to this side. We call it front of house and back of house."

"But how's that possible?" he said. "What stops other people doing what we just did?"

"It's enchanted—a Permission Wall. Only someone with the Firemark can pass through."

Archie reached out his hand to touch the invisible wall that separated the two halves of the room. His fingers met no resistance, but Bramble grabbed his hand.

"Don't do that," she said. "The people on the other side will be alarmed if they see a hand appear from nowhere!"

Archie gazed around him at the large, comfortable armchairs and sofas covered in scuffed leather. He took an instant liking to Quill's. It had a wonderful lived-in feeling. For someone who didn't like old things, Archie surprised himself.

At that moment, he spotted the auburn-haired girl who had come in at the same time as them. She hadn't vanished into thin air; she had just passed through the Door Ray. On this side of the room there were lots of teen-agers seated at tables. But there were some older people, too. The room buzzed with conversations.

"So is everyone in here an apprentice at the museum?" asked Archie.

"Yes, or they work there."

The wooden bar extended from the front of Quill's through the Permission Wall and into the back of house. Pink moved along the bar, passing effortlessly between the two sides. As she did, Archie noticed that her hair changed color from black to pink.

Pink smiled. "So, first time in the museum, eh, Arch? Better get you there in style then. The Box Seats?"

Bramble smiled. "Yes, good idea."

"And what can I get you to drink?"

"How about a Shot-in-the-Dark? It's one of my favorites," said Bramble. "With extra zing, please. He'll have the same," she added, gesturing toward Archie.

Pink turned to a wooden cabinet. The shelves were full of old-fashioned medicine bottles with stoppers. Pink took down a red bottle and dripped two drops of a thick, crimson fluid into a glass. Next, she took down a blue bottle and drizzled a small amount of a clear liquid into the glass. Finally, she took down a black bottle and added the tiniest drip. The concoction made a cackling sound and began to throw off a thick white vapor.

"Fruit shots or a choc-tail?" Pink asked.

"Fruit shots," said Bramble.

Pink held the smoking glass under one of the taps and pulled down on the porcelain handle, releasing a red liquid with a fragrant raspberry aroma.

"What's that?" Archie asked Bramble.

"It's a Motion Potion. This one is called a Shot-in-the-Dark, but there are lots of different types."

She saw the quizzical look on Archie's face.

"You need a Motion Potion to enter Mothballs."

Archie was about to ask why when Bramble held up her finger to silence him.

"You'll see."

She handed Archie his glass and waited while Pink made another for her; then she led the way through to a small nook. At one end, a red-and-gold curtain was pulled across another smaller alcove. The room was busy, but Archie spotted two empty seats at a table. He sat down.

"I wouldn't sit there if I were you," cautioned Bramble. "I mean, unless you want to go to the Lost Books section. These are the Seats of Learning. Different seats take you to different parts of Mothballs."

"Oh," said Archie. "How can you tell which ones go where?"

"Well, you can't really unless you know, so it's best not to sit down at first. The Seats of Learning are a bit unpredictable at the best of times."

They stepped back into the middle of the room, where they had a good view. "See that girl over there?" Bramble whispered, indicating the girl with auburn hair. "That's Meredith Merrydance. She works in the Mortal Magic Department with me. She came in just before us, so she will be going any second."

As Archie watched, Meredith sat down in a high-backed monk's chair at the far end of the room.

"She's sitting in the Warlock's Rest, which will take her to the Mortal Magic Department."

"Yes," said Archie. "But I still don't see how that is going to get her into—"

"Shhhh! Just watch and learn," hissed Bramble. "She's drinking her Motion Potion. Now watch what happens next."

As Archie watched, the monk's chair that Meredith was sitting in suddenly tipped backward and disappeared into the wall. One minute it was there. The next it was gone—and Meredith with it. Archie stared in disbelief.

"How . . . ? What . . . ? Who . . . ?"

Bramble grinned. "I told you it was good. Now keep watching."

Archie was still getting over his initial shock when suddenly the monk's chair reappeared. Or at least an identical chair appeared in its place. But this one was empty.

Archie rubbed his eyes. "That's incredible!" he exclaimed.

Bramble grinned. "Pretty cool, eh? Now, I think it's our turn, so we'd better sit down."

Archie glanced across at the bar and saw Pink looking over in their direction. Bramble pulled back the plush curtain. "These are the Box Seats," she said, indicating a row of seats concealed there.

"Quickly," she urged, stepping inside and gesturing for Archie to follow.

They were now in what resembled a box at the theater, with a row of faded velvet seats in a line. She closed the curtain, and they were engulfed in darkness. Archie heard Bramble's voice in his ear.

"Now, when I count to three, you must drain the glass. Every last drop, mind, or the Motion Potion won't work. Oh, and you'd better fasten your seat belt!"

Archie found a buckle in the arm of the chair and fastened it with a click. He sniffed the liquid in his glass.

It smelled of bubble gum. He was just trying to figure out what the other flavors were when he heard . . .

"One, two, three!"

Something chinked against his glass.

"Bottoms up!"

Archie tipped the contents of the glass down his throat. It tasted of wild berries and a hint of citrus. As the liquid slipped down, he felt a warm glow spreading down his arms and legs. His fingers and toes tingled pleasantly.

He was just thinking that he wouldn't mind another glass, when the floor suddenly disappeared and he felt himself falling.

The chair, with him still on it, was plunging through the floor at an alarming speed. He was thrown sideways and was taken forward with a jerking motion. He clung to the chair and closed his eyes, feeling dizzy. When he opened them again, he was rushing along a tunnel. Huge wooden shaft props held up the ceiling, and lanterns hanging from the roof lit the way. When he looked down, he was surprised to see that the chair was flying.

Just ahead, he could see Bramble's chair, skittering around and throwing up sparks into the gloom every time it touched the side of the tunnel. She was swinging her long legs and raising her hat in the air and whooping with delight every time they went around a sharp bend. Just as Archie was beginning to relax, the tunnel ended abruptly, and still in their seats, he and Bramble hurtled through a huge, cavernous space. A whooshing sound filled Archie's ears.

So I'm flying through an underground cavern in an old theater seat, he thought to himself.

The walls around him were lined with bookcases—row after row of them crammed with scrolls and the spines of old books. They reached high above him and all the way to the ground far below.

The Box Seats spiraled down and around like a corkscrew, jolting Archie from side to side. He guessed they must be a long way underground by now. Below him he could see what looked like a flock of birds, swooping in a big arc toward him. He ducked as one of them missed him by inches.

A light shone ahead in the gloom. The Box Seats flew toward it and squeezed through a narrow space before coming to a halt in a very long corridor.

"Where are we?" Asked Archie.

"The Happy Landing, of course," cried Bramble. "It's the main entrance to the museum. Now, hop out quick, or you'll be flying back to Quill's."

The first Box Seat was already moving again, rising into the air and spiraling back toward where they'd come from. Archie climbed unsteadily to his feet. His chair immediately gave a lurch and whooshed up into the air again.

At the end of the passageway was a stone arch with an oak door almost ten feet tall. The symbol of a flame was etched into the burnished wood in gold. Bramble heaved the door open.

"Welcome to the Museum of Magical Miscellany!"

CHAPTER 13

The Museum of
Magical Miscellany

Bramble took a lit torch from a bracket by the door and held it aloft. As if in answer, the other torches began to burn brighter, and Archie got his first sight of the Museum of Magical Miscellany.

Bramble beamed at him proudly. "This is the Great Gallery," she said, gesturing at the magnificent high-ceilinged room. The floor was covered with a huge mosaic with the design of a flame in the center.

On each side, sweeping wooden staircases led up to smaller galleries. The walls were packed with bookcases that reached from the floor to the ceiling.

The museum was a hive of activity. Everywhere

Archie looked there were apprentices at work in the galleries. Some were seated at little tables examining books,
while others were balanced on huge ladders with wheels
that enabled them to reach the highest shelves. Others
were pushing small carts piled high with books, or carrying books in their arms.

Something flapped overhead and then landed with a
thump on a table next to Archie. With a shock he realized
it wasn't a bird at all—it was a book! The book rested for
a second and then, opening its cover like wings, flew up
onto a nearby bookshelf and nuzzled its way into a row.

"Did you see that?" he asked Bramble.

Bramble chuckled. "Yes, there's an enchantment on the
museum that allows some of the books to move around. It
saves a lot of unnecessary work for the apprentices."

So that was what he had seen earlier.

"But I thought no one was allowed to practice magic
anymore?"

"It's against the Lore to practice magic *outside* of Mothballs and a few other magical premises, but it is permitted
inside. Mind you, it's only the books that have been here a
long time that are permitted to file themselves. They have
a special stamp that lets them fly."

As Bramble was talking, a large white book swooped

out of the air and landed on her head. "Hello, my beauty," she said to the book, which flapped its cover a few times and then was still. Bramble took it off her head. "An old friend," she said. "I filed her the first day of my apprenticeship, and she still remembers."

She placed the white book on the table. "There!" She smiled. Then, turning to Archie, she said, "Now let me show you something."

As Bramble led him through the Great Gallery, Archie's eyes were out on stalks, looking out for magic.

On one side of the room there was a long table covered in a thick black velvet cloth. Several strange objects were laid out carefully on the table in a glass case. They looked like old-fashioned scientific instruments.

"Wow!" Archie breathed excitedly.

"Astroscopes." Bramble smiled. "Magical instruments. They were part of Alexander's collection—made in the Golden Age of Magic."

Archie's eye was drawn to a magnifying glass with a silver handle. It had the most exquisite motif of a tree etched into it, and the lens was tinted pink. Bramble saw him looking at it.

"That's an Imagining Glass. It magnifies your imagination," she explained. "They are very rare indeed. An

Imagining Glass helps you get a different perspective on whatever you look at—very useful for solving problems.

"Now come along," she said, practically dragging Archie away from the table. "There's something else I want to show you."

They crossed the main gallery and climbed a marble staircase. Bramble strode on until they reached a large and very ornate set of double doors, with a golden quill set into the wood in fine marquetry.

Bramble pushed open the doors.

"The Scriptorium," she declared.

The air smelled musty, as if the room had not been opened for a long time. As Archie stepped over the threshold, torches in brackets on the wall suddenly ignited in a blaze of light.

In the center of the room were rows of high desks, each shrouded in a white dust sheet. Archie sensed that he was trespassing on the stillness of the Scriptorium.

"No one has used it in centuries, of course," said Bramble. "But everything is ready."

"Ready for what?" Archie asked.

"For the magic writers. The Flame Keepers believe that one day they will return to rewrite all the magic. When Barzak set fire to the Great Library of Alexandria and corrupted the magical books, there was nothing our ancestors could do except try to preserve them until they can be rewritten and restored to their former glory."

"But what's stopping the museum from rewriting the magic books now?" Archie asked.

Bramble laughed. "There haven't been any great magic writers for hundreds of years. Some people are still born with magical gifts—there are some at the museum, like Gideon Hawke in Lost Books, but they can't hold a candle to the old ones. They certainly aren't good enough to rewrite the magic themselves. All they can do is identify magic books and understand spells.

"When the magic writers return, there'll be another Golden Age. Until that day, the Scriptorium gathers dust."

Archie gazed around the room. Against one wall he noticed a large book with a brown leather cover. He felt himself drawn to it.

"That's *The Book of Yore*," said Bramble. "It contains the history of magic. But it's best not to disturb the past.

"This is what I wanted to show you," she said, pointing to the far end of the Scriptorium, where a huge glass dome stood surrounded by a wooden frame. "Come up here so you can see better."

She led Archie up a short flight of stairs to a raised

wooden platform that offered a better view. They were standing now above the dome, looking down on it.

Bramble's eyes sparkled in the torchlight. "Behold, the Books of Destiny!" she whispered.

As Archie gazed down through the glass, he could see there were two marble plinths. On each plinth a book was displayed at an angle of forty-five degrees. One of the books was closed, but the other, which was as big as a small table, was open.

"The Books of Destiny are different from the other magic books," explained Bramble. "They foretell the future. The closed book is *The Book of Prophecy*. It contains predictions about the future."

"What's the other book?" asked Archie, indicating the open one. From where they stood, he could see it had a somber black cover. Suspended in the center of the book was a strange crystal hourglass. The hourglass was protected by a silver case, which formed part of the spine, and the pages of the book were shaped around it so that it was visible when the book was open. But strangest of all, a blue quill floated in the air just above its open leaves. He watched in wonder as the quill danced in the air, scribbling entries.

"That is *The Book of Reckoning*," whispered Bramble.

"It keeps the tally between life and death. Each and every one of us will pass through its pages."

Archie could see that the blue quill was moving in a smooth and controlled way, as new names appeared on one side of the ledger.

"*The Book of Reckoning* contains the entry of every birth and death in the history of the world," Bramble continued. "The magic quill is from a Bennu bird, and it is constantly updating itself."

Archie gazed at the huge book in awe. "That's amazing!" he breathed.

"Yes." Bramble nodded. "That is remarkable enough, but *The Book of Reckoning* also has another purpose. It foretells the time when all the magic books will release their magic. According to legend, that day will mark either the beginning of a new Golden Age of Magic or the start of another Dark Age!

"See the hourglass in its spine?" Bramble said, pointing at the crystal hourglass Archie had noticed earlier. "It keeps a tally of the time that is left until the final reckoning."

Bramble saw the worried look on Archie's face. "Don't worry," she chuckled. "The sand in the hourglass hasn't moved for more than a thousand years."

"And what does that mean exactly?" asked Archie.

"It means that we can all sleep easy in our beds," said Bramble. "Now, come on, or you'll be late for Old Zeb. See you this afternoon."

They turned to go, and as they did, neither of them saw the single grain of sand that fell from the upper chamber of the hourglass.

CHAPTER 14

Strange Voices

It was already nine o'clock when Archie stepped back through the shaft of light into the front of Quill's. An old woman looked up from her table, surprised to see a young boy suddenly appear from the shadows at the back of the café. But then she resumed eating her cake and didn't think any more of it.

Archie crossed the courtyard to the Aisle of White. He pushed on the door, and the bell clanged behind him. Marjorie Gudge was asleep at the shop counter.

"Mrs. Gudge?" he said. "Are you all right?"

He put his hand on her shoulder and gave her a gentle shake.

"Wuzzat?" she snorted. "Geoffrey—is that you? Where've you been all this time?"

"No, it isn't Mr. Screech," said Archie. "It's me—Archie Greene. I brought a book here yesterday. Remember?"

Marjorie sat up and rubbed her eyes. "Archie Greene?" she said. "Oh yes, you're the new apprentice, aren't you? Better get you down to the workshop."

Archie looked around curiously at the bookshelves. "Are all these books magic?" he asked.

"Oh, no," said Marjorie. "The magic ones aren't for sale. They go on the bookcase behind the curtain until they are ready to go down to the workshop."

She bustled through the curtain, and Archie followed.

"So what happens to them?" he asked.

Marjorie smiled. "There's a procedure that has to be followed," she said. "Mr. Screech is very particular about it. When a book first arrives, it is inspected for damage—can't have them leaking their magic all over the place. And then it has to be cataloged and classified before it can go in the museum. Unless it is a very special book—then it might be locked in the Crypt for safekeeping."

"The book I brought in yesterday," Archie said thoughtfully, "is it special?"

"I don't think so, dear," said Marjorie. "The only

Special Instruction Mr. Screech was expecting was the almanac."

"But the man from Folly and Catchpole said my book had a Special Instruction, too," said Archie.

"Really?" said Marjorie. "Well, he must have been mistaken."

"But it was written on a scroll in a strange language. He translated it."

"Well, I'm afraid he must have mistranslated it," said Marjorie. "I'm not surprised. Some of those old magical languages are very confusing."

Archie felt a pang of disappointment. "Oh," he said. Horace Catchpole must have got it wrong. It wasn't a Special Instruction after all. Archie shrugged. "Can I have it back then?"

Marjorie smiled. "Absolutely not! It's a tradition— every new apprentice brings a book. It's called a Snook. It's a way of making sure that the apprentice is worthy. Now, let's get you down to the workshop."

The shop doorbell interrupted her. "Wait here while I serve this customer. And don't touch anything."

But Archie was no longer listening to her. He could hear a rustling noise from the bookcase where the magical books were kept. At first it sounded like the pages of a newspaper being turned, but as he listened, Archie could hear a voice.

"It's not safe here!" it rustled. "Something is stealing my magic."

Archie froze. He peered at the bookcase to see where the sound was coming from, and as he did, he heard an answering voice. The second voice sounded like tissue paper crinkling.

"My magic is fading, too!" it sighed sadly. "Something is taking it all. I will not last much longer."

Archie turned his head. The second voice was coming from the top shelf of the bookcase. He stepped closer and put his ear to a little book with a red cover.

"Who are you?" he asked.

Silence. Archie waited a few seconds. "I know you are there," he said, lowering his voice. "I heard you whispering!"

The tissue-paper voice spoke again.

"You can hear us?" it asked, a note of surprise in its crinkly voice.

"Yes, of course," Archie said, less certain.

"He can hear us!" exclaimed the first voice—the one that rustled like a newspaper.

There was an excited murmuring of papery voices.

"He can hear us!" they twittered among themselves. "He can hear us!"

"Yes," said Archie. "And it's not the first time either. It was your voices I heard yesterday when I came into the bookshop. Why wouldn't I hear you?"

The first voice answered. It was coming from a chunky green book on the shelf below the little red book. "Most humans can't hear us," it explained. "In fact, you are the first one in years!"

Archie could hear lots of other papery voices murmuring now. The bookcase seemed to be alive with them. They sounded like little birds twittering in a hedge.

"What about the other apprentices?" Archie demanded.

"No," said a new voice that was deeper than the first two and sounded stiff like parchment. "They can't hear us. Only you can hear us. You have the gift!"

"What gift?" Archie asked suspiciously.

"You are a book whisperer!" exclaimed tissue-paper voice. "Some people can hear magic books talk to one another and can talk to them. It's very rare, though. There hasn't been a book whisperer for a long, long time. And because you are the only one who can hear us, you might be the only one who can help us!"

"Hold on a minute," said Archie, who couldn't quite believe his ears. "How do I know this isn't some sort of trick?"

"A trick?" the little red book crinkled, dismayed. "Dark scribes did not make me. I am a book of blessings. My magic is wrought from kind words. I am full of wise sayings, and I have one for you, Archie Greene. Listen carefully.

"Release the magic that lies within.
Believe in its power above all things."

"Thank you," said Archie, surprised that the book knew his name. "But what does it mean?"

"That is for you to discover," said the little red book. "It is my blessing to you. My magic is almost gone. Something has taken it all."

"What is this thing that is stealing your magic?"

There was much murmuring and whispering among the books. It seemed to Archie that there was some sort of disagreement going on. Eventually, newspaper voice spoke up.

"It is dark magic that is feeding on our magic!"

Archie felt a sense of dread. He remembered that

Bramble had warned him about the Greaders coming to Oxford, and how it was a sign that dark magic was present.

The rustling voices grew louder. Archie could tell they were arguing.

"Shhhhh—we have said too much!" warned parchment voice, which was coming from a big blue book. "Do not speak of it! It will hear us and punish us!"

The rustling stopped. The voices fell silent. Archie stared at the blue book. Its title was written on its spine. *Magical Leadership: The Pragmatic Approach.*

Just then Marjorie's head appeared through the curtain.

"Come along, dear! Do get a move on. We mustn't keep Old Zeb waiting."

She ushered him along the dingy corridor. All the while he was thinking about what the magic books had told him. He wondered if his book could talk, and whether it was safe from whatever was frightening the others.

Marjorie stopped at the top of the stairs and handed him a lantern. "Third door on the right," she said. "No other."

CHAPTER 15

Bookbinding for Beginners

Down in the Mending Workshop, Old Zeb was perched on a wooden stool at the workbench, his cheeks flushed red. His lips puckered and creased as he whistled a jaunty tune. When he saw Archie, he smiled.

"You're late. Never mind, you're here now. Try to be on time tomorrow. We've got a lot to do."

Archie looked around him. The workshop was larger than he remembered, and the smell of old parchment was even stronger. He noticed a vise on the side of the bench and a large book press beside it.

"First things first," Old Zeb said, holding up a finger to get his attention. "You'll be needing your own tool kit.

I'll get you started, and then you'll have to acquire the other bits as you go along. Have a word with one of the apprentices in Natural Magic—they might be able to help."

He winked and reached under the bench.

"One pair of gloves—for the handling of dangerous books," he said, producing what looked like a pair of scaly green oven mitts. Archie wondered what they were made from. It looked like alligator skin, only much thicker. Could it be dragon skin?

"One magical needle, very hard to come by—this one is made from a werewolf's claw," said the old bookbinder, holding up a large, black, hooked object.

"One reel of thread—finest yeti hair.

"One binder's knife—forged in the Flame of Pharos. And finally," he said, placing a brown pouch-like bag on the bench, "your very own magic tool bag. It's resistant to magic, so it will stop all but the very strongest spells from leaking out—ideal for carrying damaged books and unknown magical objects."

The old man smiled at Archie.

"Oh, almost forgot—you might need this." He put a small brass key-shaped object on the bench.

"What is it?" asked Archie, hoping it might also be magical.

"It's a key to the shop—so you can let yourself in if you need to."

Archie smiled and put the key in his pocket.

"Now then," the old bookbinder continued, "this morning we'll cover the basics."

He hopped off his stool and took down a large book from a bookcase. He laid it on the bench. Archie saw that it was entitled *A Beginner's Guide to Magic*.

"Is this a . . . magic book?" Archie asked, his eyes wide in awe.

"Good heavens, no," said the old man. "It's just a magic reference book."

He opened the book to a page divided into three sections. "First," he said, "what do you know about the different types of magic?"

Archie's face fell. "Er, not a lot," he said. "I only found out there was magic yesterday."

"You didn't know about magic!" exclaimed Old Zeb. He shook his head sadly. "What do they teach children in schools these days?

"Well, never mind, you'll soon catch up," he added more brightly. "All you need to know for now is that there are three types of magic."

He tapped the page with his finger. "The first is

Natural Magic. That's the purest kind and comes from magical plants and creatures—unicorns, dragons et cetera, et cetera—and the elemental forces of nature—the sun, the stars, and so on. The symbol for Natural Magic is a lightning bolt in a tree," he added.

"Mortal Magic is the second kind of magic and is man-made magic. It includes the magical instruments and other devices used by magicians to channel magical power. It is usually represented by a crystal ball," he said, pointing at the symbol on the open page.

"And finally," he said, gesturing to a smiling skull, "there is Supernatural Magic, which uses the power of supernatural beings. That includes the use of good and bad spirits, genies, demons, and anything else that's not of this world."

The old bookbinder paused. "Supernatural Magic is usually regarded as the darkest of the three. But any one of them can be dangerous."

Archie stared at the three symbols. He had seen them somewhere before, but where? With a start, he remembered. They had appeared in the window of the clasp on his book. The clasp had another symbol, too, of a matchstick figure with a crescent crown. He wondered what that symbol meant.

Old Zeb moved on quickly. "Each of the three branches of magic has its own department in the museum. Dr. Motley Brown is the current head of Natural Magic." He pointed at a photograph of a short man in a tweed suit. "Vincent von Herring is head of Mortal Magic," he said, indicating a tall man wearing a pink bow tie. "And that," he said, pointing to a slender woman with long silver hair, "is Feodora Graves, head of Supernatural Magic.

"Every apprentice learns the three basic skills for protecting magic books—Book Finding, Bookbinding, and Book Minding. And every apprentice spends time working in all three branches of magic. Any questions so far?"

"Does everyone start in Bookbinding?" Archie asked.

"No," said Old Zeb. "The Flame decides the order in which you learn. Every apprentice has his or her own path to follow. Not many start with binding, though," he added, looking thoughtful.

"It's the hardest of the three skills, you see. Only the most gifted of the apprentices start with it. Wolfus Bone— he works in Lost Books now—Arthur Ripley, and your father, too. I taught all three of 'em. The only one I didn't teach is Gideon Hawke."

So it was true, his father had learned Bookbinding from Old Zeb. Archie felt a surge of pride that he was following a family tradition.

Old Zeb was talking again. "Now there's just a couple more things you need to know. The Lores—they're all up there, all five of 'em." He pointed at a sign on the wall.

He read aloud.

"The First Lore states that all magical books and artifacts must be returned to the Museum of Magical Miscellany for inspection and classification." He looked at Archie. "No ifs, ands, or buts—understand?"

Archie nodded.

"Good lad. The Second Lore says that magical books and artifacts may not be used or bought and sold until properly identified and classified. Self-explanatory, I think.

"The Third Lore forbids the unauthorized use of magic outside of magical premises. And the Fourth Lore says that hoarding books to accumulate power is outlored under the prohibition of dangerous practices."

Old Zeb's face turned serious. "It is our duty to make sure the magic books are safe. We can't have them falling into the wrong hands.

"Finally, the Fifth Lore says the mistreatment of magical creatures is expressly forbidden.

"Now, I want you to be on your guard, because we

suspect that Greaders are operating in Oxford. Professor von Herring will tell you more about that at the apprentices' meeting tomorrow. You know about the meeting, I take it?"

"My cousin said something about it," Archie replied.

"Good." Old Zeb nodded. "Make sure you attend.

"Well, that's enough theory for one day." The old man rubbed his hands together like an excited child. "Right, let's get on to the practical stuff. See these books here?"

He indicated two bookshelves on the wall above the workbench. "Everything you need to know is in these books," he said.

Archie scanned the bookshelves. There were several books about bookbinding and repairing spells, but the one that caught his eye was called *Magic Collectors Past & Present*. He was going to ask about it, but Old Zeb drew his attention to a volume called *Bookbinding for Beginners* by Basil Gumtree.

"I was apprenticed to Basil Gumtree myself," the old man said, shaking his head fondly. "Best bookbinder I've ever seen. Course I was a young lad then, starting out on my apprenticeship just like you."

"Yes, well, about that," said Archie, feeling awkward. "Do you really think I'm the right person to be your apprentice? I mean, I appreciate the offer and everything, but I don't know the first thing about magical books, or magic for that matter. Are you sure you aren't making a mistake?"

"Mistake?" The old man's brow creased. "Impossible! The Flame decides, and the Flame chose you. The mark of the Flame is binding. Bookbinding, in this case!" he added with a grin.

He gave Archie a knowing wink. "You are my apprentice, and that's the end of it. Now let's get on with our work. The books won't bind themselves!" he said, his face breaking into a smile, then immediately turning serious. "Actually, sometimes they do! Some of them can't be trusted, you see."

Later that morning, Archie and Old Zeb were sitting on their tall stools at the end of the long bench. At the other end were two piles of books, labeled "Pop-Ups" and "Pop-Outs." Archie regarded them curiously, thinking about the pop-up storybooks Gran used to read him.

"I see you have an eye for the Poppers." Old Zeb grinned. "But be careful with those. There's no telling what might pop out of them! Now let's see what else we've got. Pass me that brown book over there."

Archie picked up a book that smelled earthy.

"A Natural Magic book," Old Zeb explained. "Written by the magician who tended the Hanging Gardens of Babylon."

The old man peered at it through a large magnifying glass. "Quite straightforward," he said. "Couple of small rips in the cover—look like they were made by rose thorns. And it's shedding some of its leaves. Nothing that some manure and a drink of water won't fix!"

The old bookbinder picked up a small hole punch and a hammer and made two holes in the book's spine. Then he took a large needle that looked like a hook for catching very large fish and threaded it with green gardening twine. With surprising speed the old man stitched the loose pages back, carefully knotting the twine before cutting off the end with some garden shears.

Next, he applied some glue from a small pot on the workbench to the tears in the cover. Then, to Archie's surprise, he picked up a battered old watering can and liberally sprinkled it with water.

"Nearly done," he muttered. "Just needs a bit of manure. Stick it in that bucket over there," he added, pointing to an old wooden one in a corner of the workshop.

"Yes, that's it," he added when Archie looked unsure.

"Just bury it deep in the muck. Be good as new in no time."

Archie gave him a quizzical glance but realized that he was completely serious.

"Right," said Old Zeb. "I'm just stepping out for a moment to see if Marjorie has anything urgent for me. Won't be long. Finish what you're doing and have a cup of tea. Don't touch anything else."

The old bookbinder opened the workshop door and stepped out, whistling his way along the passageway. Archie picked up the bucket. He plunged the gardening book into the manure, being careful not to get it on his hands. The book had a sweet smell like magnolia blossom. He smiled to himself. He felt a bit silly burying a book in manure.

When he was finished, he collected the teacups from the workbench, and he was just putting the kettle on the stove to boil when he caught sight of the Poppers.

Archie felt a little surge of curiosity. He glanced over at the door. What harm could it do to have a quick peek as long as he was careful?

He turned his head sideways, reading the spines. One in particular caught his eye, *Medieval Magic: Charming Knights.*

Archie opened the book and ran his eye down the table

of contents. The names of various knights were listed. Halfway down he spotted Sir Bodwin the Bold. His coat of arms was a roaring lion, and the reference said he was the bravest knight in all of England. Archie opened the book to the page, expecting a three-dimensional image to pop up.

Sure enough, out popped a parchment knight in full armor seated on a black horse. Archie couldn't see anything magic about it. He noticed that the parchment was torn so that Sir Bodwin, instead of sitting up straight on his horse, was tilted at an angle, as if he was falling out of his saddle. It made the knight look rather comical.

Only a small repair was needed, and Archie couldn't resist giving it a try. He took Old Zeb's needle and put in a stitch that pulled Sir Bodwin back into an upright position. He stood back and admired his handiwork just as the kettle started to whistle.

He was taking the kettle off the heat with his back to the Popper when he detected a sulfurous smell, like a match being struck. There was a loud popping sound behind him, followed by the whinnying of a horse.

"Steady, girl," said a man's voice.

For a moment, Archie didn't trust himself to turn around.

When he did, he couldn't believe his eyes. Standing in the workshop, with its tail swishing and its nostrils flaring, was a full-size black warhorse clad in silver armor. Mounted on the horse was a knight, also in full armor, with a red plume sticking out from his iron helmet and a crest of a lion. He was so tall on his steed that his plume touched the ceiling of the workshop. In his hand, the knight held a sword with a gleaming blade. He had his visor open, revealing a thickly bearded chin, and was making a clicking noise with his tongue against the roof of his mouth, so the horse's ears twitched.

Archie knew they must have popped up from the book, but for a moment he could only stare. The magic he'd seen at Quill's and the museum had been impressive, but this was something else. Archie felt goose bumps on his skin.

Then the knight spoke.

"Well met, young sir," he said, and he raised his gauntlet-clad hand in a salute. "I am Sir Bodwin the Bold. You have rendered me a great service. I've been stuck at that angle for years—very uncomfortable. But now I am restored to my former glory, thanks to you. What is your name?"

"Ar-Archie Greene," Archie stuttered, staring at the

knight. He knew it was rude, but he couldn't help it.

"I am at your service, Archie Greene," Sir Bodwin said, bowing so low that the plume in his helmet almost tickled Archie's nose. "How can I repay you for your noble deed?"

"Urm . . . you really don't have to," said Archie, not sure what else to say.

The knight continued, "It's very embarrassing being a knight when everyone laughs at you. But now I can hold my head up high once more—literally! I am forever in your debt. What quest would you have me fulfill?"

Archie was desperately racking his brain for a response when the door to the workshop opened and Old Zeb's face appeared.

To Archie's immense relief, the old bookbinder did not seem in the least put out to find a very large horse and a fully armed knight in his workshop. In fact, he just laughed.

"Been at the Poppers, I see, then, young Archie?" he said. "I warned you about that!"

Archie opened his mouth to reply, but at that moment a steaming pile of horse dung landed on the ground next to his foot. Old Zeb chuckled at the sight of it. Relieved, Archie laughed with him.

The knight raised his hand in salute. "Well met," he said cheerily. "I am Sir Bodwin the Bold. My sword is at this boy's service."

"Well, that's very kind, I'm sure," Old Zeb replied, "but he doesn't need your help just now."

He reached into his pocket and produced a small glass phial. He pointed it at the knight and removed the stopper. A wispy white vapor drifted out and coiled around Sir Bodwin and his steed. There was a crackling noise like static electricity as the white mist was sucked back into the phial, taking the knight and his horse with it. Old Zeb immediately replaced the glass bottle's top.

Archie blinked. Sir Bodwin and his horse were gone. All that was left to show they had ever been there was the steaming pile of horse dung.

Old Zeb raised his eyebrows knowingly.

"There, now," he chided. "Let that be a lesson to you, young Archie."

Archie felt the color rise to his cheeks. "How did you get rid of them? Where did they go?" he asked.

"I phialed 'em away, of course!" said Old Zeb, grinning. "With my Popper Stopper," he added with a twinkle in his eye. "All the Museum Elders have them. Don't know where we'd be without them. Well, yes I do, we'd be overrun with Poppers. That's where we'd be!"

Archie smiled. "I think I'd like to get one," he said, eyeing the glass bottle.

"Not allowed." The old man smiled. "First and Second Hand apprentices are strictly forbidden from carrying them. Third Hands, with three Firemarks, are allowed to use them under supervision. Makes it too easy, you see, to start opening Poppers without due care and attention. Far too dangerous."

Old Zeb placed the glass phial on a shelf. "That will have to go back to the museum later, but it will be safe enough there for now."

Archie looked at the horse dung on the floor of the workshop.

The old bookbinder grinned again. "Right," he said. "Now get a shovel and clear that up—it'll work terrifically on that gardening book. And I'll take the rest home for my tomatoes!"

A Visitor

Later that afternoon, when Archie had finished at the bookshop, he met Bramble outside Quill's. As they walked home, he told her about Sir Bodwin.

"So, you found out about Poppers, then?" she said with a giggle.

"Yes, you could say that," Archie said, feeling a little foolish. "But it was worth it. It was absolutely fantastic!"

"Yes," said Bramble. "But be careful with them. Poppers can get you into trouble. There was an unfortunate incident a few years ago involving a rhinoceros and a china shop. Actually, it was more a priceless collection of porcelain. Quite a big one."

"And the rhinoceros?" Archie asked.

"Yes, that was quite a big one as well. It lasted three days, and there wasn't a single piece of china left."

Archie raised his eyebrows. "Smashing!" He chuckled.

Bramble grinned. "Exactly, but it caused a bit of a fuss at the time, and Dad got into a lot of trouble."

"You mean Uncle Woodbine let the Popper out?" exclaimed Archie.

Bramble pulled a face. "Yes, 'fraid so," she said. "That's why he doesn't work at the museum anymore. He had to leave after that."

Archie looked thoughtful. There was more to his uncle Woodbine than met the eye. "What does he do now?" he asked.

"He's a Finder. Most of the jobs at the museum are for Minders—they look after the magic books and keep them safe. There are a few Binders, like Old Zeb. Then there are Finders, who get paid for any lost magic books they find. That's why we collect the old books."

"I see," said Archie. "And that was all because of a Popper?"

"Yes," said Bramble, "but it's the Drawing Books that you really need to look out for. They are the most dangerous of all."

"How can a Drawing Book be dangerous?" asked Archie incredulously.

Bramble ignored his skeptical tone. "Trust me, they can. Drawing Books draw you in," she said. "You can end up being a character in the story."

"That's weird!" said Archie.

"It's more than weird," cautioned Bramble. "You can end up trapped forever and unable to escape. This isn't a lark, Archie. Some magic books are not very nice at all! You'll find out more at the meeting about dark magic tomorrow, I'm sure. Mum's given me a Keep Safe, because she says you can never be too careful with Greaders around."

She showed Archie a gold charm bracelet around her wrist. It had a tiny heart, an anchor, and a bow and arrow. "It's a magical gift that protects you. I got it when I started my apprenticeship."

"Do you think we're in danger then?" Archie asked.

Bramble shrugged. "Better to be safe than sorry."

When they got back to Houndstooth Road, Loretta met them in the hall.

"Good timing. You've got a visitor, Archie. Says he got our address from Granny Greene."

Archie and Bramble went through to the kitchen to find Horace Catchpole drinking elderberry squash with Thistle.

"There's something you should know," Horace exclaimed when he saw Archie. "There's a second message. It was added later. It should have been delivered with the package and the first scroll, but somehow it got overlooked."

"What does it say?" asked Archie.

"It's in Enochian script," said Horace, "the language of angels." From his pocket he produced a scroll tied with a bottle-green ribbon. He opened it on the table. "The language of angels is the purest magical language of all. Several of the great books of magic were written in it, including the *Opus Magus*. But it's even more obscure than Alphabet of the Magi, the magical language the first message was written in. It's a devil to translate."

Archie didn't have the heart to tell Horace that he'd gotten the first translation wrong.

Horace continued, "Anyway, it's a riddle."

"You mean you don't know what to make of it?" asked Thistle.

Horace pulled a face. "Well, no, it really is a riddle. It rhymes and everything."

"I see," said Archie, wondering whether Horace's translation could be trusted after the last one.

Horace straightened his glasses, and referring to his notebook, he began to read. Bramble grabbed a pen and started transcribing what was being translated.

"Buried deep in caverns cold
A secret that remains untold
Two ancient sentries guard the prize
With lion heart and eagle eyes."

Archie gazed at the scroll. As Horace read out the words, the strange letters began to shimmer and rearrange themselves into words that he could understand. He rubbed his eyes.

"What does the second verse say, Horace?" asked Thistle.

Horace continued,

"In stony silence shadows sleep
The final gift is safe to keep
To pass requires a simple test . . ."

But it was Archie who finished the verse.

"Name the one whom I served best."

The other three stared at him.

"How did you know that?" gasped Horace. "It took me hours to translate it, and you got it in seconds. Who taught you to read magical languages?"

Archie felt confused and embarrassed. "It must have been a fluke," he said, but he knew that no one believed it. He didn't even believe it himself.

"What does the riddle mean?" he asked, trying to change the subject.

"Beats me." Horace shrugged. "But I thought you'd want to know about it. It goes with the first scroll and package, but it was sent after they were."

"Who sent it?" Bramble asked impatiently.

"We can't read his name in our records," confided Horace. "The ink is smudged. But we do know that he was a magician."

"A magician!" exclaimed Archie. "I wonder if that's who sent me the book as well!"

Horace shrugged. "And the scroll has this weird symbol on it," he added, holding it out so they could all see.

"Does that mean anything to you?"

"Yes," said Archie slowly. "It's the same one as on the clasp of my book."

⌒

When Archie went up to bed that night to ponder the riddle, he found a letter on his pillow—it was from Gran! Loretta must have put it there in case he wanted to read it in private. Hungry for news, he tore it open and started to read.

Dearest Archie,

I hope you are settling in well with the Foxes.

By now you will have discovered some things that you did not know about your family and especially your father's past. You are probably wondering why I kept so much from you.

There are so many things that I should have told you. But your father made me promise to keep you away from magic until you were old enough to make your own mind up. He was trying to protect you.

I write in haste because I must make a journey. There are some matters that I have to attend to. I realize now that I should have acted sooner. But what is done is done, and I cannot change it.

*I will try not to worry about you, because I
know you are in the safekeeping of the Foxes. Life
is a funny thing, because up until a few weeks ago
nothing would have worried me more!*

Loretta and Woodbine know how to reach me.

*There is one more thing I need to tell you. (I
once told your father this.) There are many different
types of courage in this world. But they all have one
thing in common. You cannot be truly courageous if
you are not truly frightened. Real courage is doing
what we know to be right even though we are afraid
for our own safety. Remember this. It will help you
be brave when the time comes.*

Love,

Gran

A postcard had been slipped in with the letter. It was
postmarked Kathmandu.

Thinking about Gran made him think about his dad's
things. He wondered whether they would be able to help
him with the riddle. He took out the shoe box that Thistle
had given him, removed the lid, and looked inside at an
assortment of his father's possessions. There was a pen,

some faded black-and-white photographs, a pair of gloves, and some books.

He picked up one of the photographs and examined it. It was a picture of a boy and girl standing together. The girl was clearly recognizable as a younger version of Loretta Foxe. She looked to be about ten. The boy was older, around Archie's age, and had to be his father. They were standing outside Quill's.

Archie put the photo back in the box and picked up one of the books. It was an old scrapbook with some newspaper cuttings. He decided to look at it later. Another book was called *Magical Greats: The Good, the Bad, & the Ugly.* It was a catalogue of all the most famous and infamous magical books ever written.

What was the book that Horace had mentioned? The *Opus Magus.* Archie looked it up in the index.

THE OPUS MAGUS: Perhaps the greatest of all the magical books, the *Opus Magus* was written during the Golden Age of Magic by an unknown hand and is said to contain the secrets of writing new magic. Once housed in the Great Library of Alexandria, it is believed that the *Opus Magus* was incinerated in the fire that destroyed the library.

Archie flicked on through the book until another entry caught his eye.

THE BOOK OF YORE: An ancient codex that contains the history of magic, including many secrets about the past. *The Book of Yore* is sometimes included with the Books of Destiny, but strictly speaking, it has no power to predict the future. Rather, the secrets it reveals about the past may alter the fates of those who discover them. *The Book of Yore* can be consulted by asking it a direct question, although what it reveals may not seem immediately relevant. The book never lies, but it has a dark side, which makes it dangerous.

Archie put the book back in the shoe box. He noticed another called *Creatures to Avoid If You Are of a Nervous Disposition* by Timothy Tremble. It was full of descriptions of all sorts of magical creatures, with drawings of dragons, unicorns, and centaurs. There were also pictures of vampires and werewolves and something called a flarewolf—a wolflike creature that breathed fire like a dragon.

Archie shivered involuntarily. The creature sounded

vile. He was still thinking about it when he fell asleep. He dreamed a fire-breathing dragon was chasing him and trying to burn his book.

CHAPTER 17

Dark Magic

The next day, Archie stood beside Bramble as one by one the other apprentices arrived for the meeting. They were in a large room in the back of Quill's Coffee & Chocolate House that was used for museum business. Chairs were arranged in neat rows facing a raised stage with a lectern.

"I can't remember another meeting like this, and we've had Greaders in Oxford before," Bramble said. "The Museum Elders must be worried."

Archie was feeling self-conscious. Most of the other apprentices were several years older than him and seemed much more sure of themselves. A tall boy of about fifteen entered the room. He had dark hair swept across his face that he kept flicking out of his eyes.

"Who's that?" Archie whispered. Bramble grinned and raised her eyebrows appreciatively.

"That's Rupert Trevallan," she whispered back. "He works in the Natural Magic Department—in the Mythical Menagerie.

"And that's Enid Drew, from Supernatural Magic," Bramble said, indicating a girl with short black hair and glasses.

She suddenly nudged him in the ribs. "Look who else is here! Your friend Arabella Ripley!"

Archie followed her gaze and spotted Arabella standing on her own by the door, with a bored look on her face.

"I wonder what she's doing here," Bramble said. "Oh look!" she exclaimed. "Meredith is talking to Rupert. I'm just going to say hello. Back in a mo."

She set off across the room with a determined look on her face. Archie watched as she kissed the auburn-haired girl on the cheek and beamed her best smile at the tall boy, whose face reddened at the sight of her.

Without Bramble at his side, Archie suddenly found himself in a roomful of strangers.

The only other person he vaguely knew was Arabella.

He tried to make eye contact to be friendly, but she ignored him. Archie felt awkward. He was just wondering whether it would be better to stand there by himself or go over and join Bramble and her friends when the door flew open and a tall man with gray hair and a silver mustache strode into the room.

He wore a dark suit with a crisply pressed white shirt and a pink bow tie. Under one arm, he carried a silver-topped walking cane. Archie recognized him from the picture Old Zeb had shown him. The man marched up onto the stage and clapped his hands to get everyone's attention. The room immediately fell silent.

"Apprentices," he said in a loud voice. "As most of you know, I am Vincent von Herring, head of Mortal Magic. I am also the chairman of the Dangerous Books Committee, and it is in that capacity that I have called this meeting today. I have done so for your own safety and for the safety of the museum.

"But before we get started, I would like to introduce two new apprentices. Archie Greene joins us as the new apprentice bookbinder." Archie felt his cheeks burning as all eyes turned to look at him. Embarrassingly, he had no control over his face, which by the way it was burning had turned a bright shade of pink. "And our second new apprentice is Arabella Ripley," Professor von Herring continued, "who joins the Supernatural Magic Department as a bookminder. The third new apprentice cannot be here today for reasons that will become apparent."

All heads swiveled to look at Arabella, who tossed her head imperiously.

"That's why she's here!" whispered Bramble, who'd come back to stand with Archie. "She must have just had her twelfth birthday. I bet her parents pulled some strings to get her an apprenticeship. She would still have to pass the Flame test, of course, but all her family have been apprentices, so it's in her blood."

"Miss Foxe, please," chided Professor von Herring, glaring at Bramble. "We are here on a matter of the utmost seriousness."

He paused to make sure he had the full attention of his audience. "As some of you may have heard, the other new apprentice was attacked outside Quill's—a boy by the name of Peter Quiggley. Luckily, he was released without serious injury. Mr. Quiggley is at home and is expected to make a full recovery. But he was held captive for several hours and was threatened by a person or persons unknown who thought he had information regarding the whereabouts of a magical book."

A hush fell on the room. From his breast pocket Professor von Herring removed some spectacles and put them on. The lenses were thick and made his brown eyes look like two trout swimming in bowls of water.

"It has also come to the attention of the museum that Geoffrey Screech, proprietor of the Aisle of White bookshop, is missing. Mr. Screech has not been seen since Monday—the same day that Mr. Quiggley was attacked. The two events may be linked. If they are, then this could well be the work of Greaders operating in Oxford. If that is the case, then they have almost certainly received information that a very powerful magic book is nearby."

There were around fifty apprentices in the room, and all of them were hanging on Professor von Herring's every word.

Von Herring peered over his spectacles with a solemn expression on his face. "There is a chance"—he paused—"that this book is one of the Terrible Tomes!"

There was a collective intake of breath. Von Herring continued.

"It is *vital* that as apprentices you understand the seriousness of this threat. There are seven Terrible Tomes in all. I will not name them all here. But I can tell you that they include the dark spell book of Hecate the witch, known as *The Grim Grimoire*, and *The Nosferu*, which was written by Vlad III, Prince of Wallachia, in the blood of his enemies."

He paused for dramatic effect. "Yes, that's right, Count Dracula himself! And that's without even mentioning the darkest of all the books of Supernatural Magic—Barzak's *Book of Souls*."

The apprentices exchanged nervous looks.

"Four of the Terrible Tomes are currently under lock and key in the museum Crypt, but three remain unaccounted for. If one of the missing Tomes should fall into the hands of a Greader, it could destroy the museum and all the magic in it."

Von Herring looked around the room. "A boy has already been attacked. If any of you have information about this matter, you must tell me immediately. Do you understand?"

The apprentices all nodded. "Good. Now are there any questions?"

There was a moment's silence, and then a voice spoke up.

"Yes, Professor. How would we recognize one of the Terrible Tomes?"

Archie turned his head to see who had asked the question. He was surprised to see that it was Arabella Ripley.

"Well, Ms. Ripley, that is an excellent question," von Herring said, his trout eyes settling upon the new apprentice. "But I am surprised that with your family connections you do not know the answer already!"

A few of the apprentices snickered nervously. Professor von Herring smiled unkindly. Arabella looked furious.

"What's the joke?" Archie whispered to Bramble.

"It's complicated. I'll tell you later," Bramble whispered back.

Von Herring was speaking again. "The answer to Ms. Ripley's question is that—as her grandfather discovered—it is almost impossible to tell the Terrible Tomes from the run-of-the-mill magical books that fill the museum book shelves. Indeed, one of the properties that the seven share is the ability to disguise themselves as seemingly unimportant books. Only if they are threatened will they momentarily drop their guard to reveal their true nature. But such glimpses are very rare and take a trained eye to spot. They are also resistant to most forms of magical security, so they have to be handled very carefully indeed.

"That is why it is vital that you report any suspicious books or behavior. Do I make myself clear?"

CHAPTER 18

Dangerous Books

As they left the room, Archie's head was buzzing with what he'd heard. All around him, the apprentices were chattering among themselves. They sounded like a swarm of excited bees. They filed out of the function room back into Quill's.

Archie was thinking about what von Herring had said about reporting anything suspicious. The books in the Aisle of White had told him that something was stealing their magic. He wondered whether he should tell someone what he knew. But it would mean explaining he was a book whisperer, and Archie doubted that anyone would believe him. Just then, Bramble grabbed his arm.

"Let's get a hot chocolate and I'll tell you about Arthur Ripley."

A few minutes later they were seated at a table with a Choc-tail and two straws.

Bramble spoke in a low voice so that she wouldn't be overheard. "Arabella's grandfather, Arthur Ripley, was head of Lost Books. He persuaded the Museum Elders to give him special powers to track down the Terrible Tomes. But it turned out he wanted them for himself.

"It was about twelve years ago now. Ripley got into the Crypt somehow and tried to take the four Terrible Tomes kept there. But he was discovered by one of the elders. A fire broke out. No one knows how it started, probably magical combustion—that can happen if a lot of magic is suddenly released. Luckily, the Crypt is enchanted, so none of the books in there were damaged. But the fire spread to other parts of the museum, and some books were destroyed. Anyway, by the time they put it out, Ripley was burned to ash. They couldn't even identify his body."

"That's grim," said Archie.

"Yes, but a lot of people thought he had it coming," said Bramble. "Arthur Ripley had made a lot of enemies.

"After that, the Dangerous Books Committee was set up, and von Herring was brought in to investigate what

Ripley had been up to. He discovered a whole load of magic books that Ripley had been hoarding."

Archie was about to ask what happened to Ripley's collection when he caught sight of a tall, stooping man talking to Professor von Herring at the bar.

"I know that man," he whispered to Bramble.

She nodded. "Yes, that's Aurelius Rusp. I wonder what he's doing here."

Rusp strode past them, his face set in an angry scowl. The two cousins watched him sweep through the Door Ray and out the main door.

"He's not very friendly," Archie observed.

"Rusp? No, he's famously unfriendly. A right old grouch, in fact. Funny that we should see him today, though, when we were just talking about Arthur Ripley, because Rusp was in the museum on the night of the fire. He was the one who discovered what was going on and raised the alarm. If it hadn't been for Rusp, the place would have burned to the ground." She paused. "He's been a bit strange ever since. Very intense."

"You think it's because of the fire?"

"Yeah, it affected him. He's always searching for books. Trying to replace the ones that got burned—that's what Dad says."

"Why would he do that?" Archie asked. "I mean, it's not as if it was his fault or anything."

Bramble shrugged. "Who knows," she said. "Perhaps he feels responsible somehow or feels he should have said something sooner. But there are other rumors, too. Some people say he's got links to the Greaders."

CHAPTER 19

The Almanac

After the incident with the Poppers, Archie assumed it would be a while before he was allowed anywhere near another magical book. But when he arrived at the Mending Workshop a couple of days later, Old Zeb had put two books on the bench. Pages had been marked in each.

"Right," said the old bookbinder. "Orders from the Elders are that we've got to speed up your lessons. With Greaders about, they want all apprentices to be ready in case of danger. Today, you'll be learning about the different types of magical books."

His serious expression dissolved into a gummy grin.

"You'll like this," he added, a gleam in his eye. "It will be fun."

The old man tapped his nose with his finger. "Since you're so fond of 'em, let's start with the Poppers. Poppers are enchanted books. They contain spells that are bound to the book until it is opened—then, ready or not, out they pop!

"There are two types—Pop-Ups and Pop-Outs. With a Pop-Up, the spell pops up but it remains with the book it came from. Once they're out, of course, it can be a devil of a job to get them back inside the book, but at least they can't wander off. So let's see a Pop-Up in action." He pointed at the first book, which had a dark-green cover and was entitled *The Dodo Bird and Other Extinct Animals.*

"Go ahead," the old bookbinder urged, "open it!"

When Archie opened the book, there was a loud popping sound, and a large and very surprised-looking woolly mammoth appeared in the room, still chewing a mouthful of grass. It had long yellow tusks and a puzzled expression on its face. Its two small eyes regarded Archie down its long trunk.

"A Popper has no idea that it is only a temporary spell, so it thinks and behaves just like a real animal or person—a mammoth in this case," Old Zeb explained. "This makes Poppers extremely realistic but potentially dangerous, because they don't want to go back into the book once they're out. That's why Popper Stoppers were invented. It allows them to be safely stored until they ezaporate—which means the spell expires or they go back into their book of their own volition.

"I hope we didn't disturb your breakfast," the old man said to the mammoth. He winked at Archie and produced an apple from his pocket and gave it to the bemused animal. Then he took out a Popper Stopper and removed the stopper to release the white mist, which immediately surrounded the mammoth. When the mist was sucked back into the glass phial, the creature disappeared with another loud *pop*.

Old Zeb handed the glass phial to Archie. "Put it with the one from the other day," he said. "It's not much of a phialing system," he added with a grin, "but it'll have to do!"

Archie smiled at his joke and placed the phial with the mammoth on the shelf next to the one containing Sir Bodwin.

"Now for the Pop-Outs. With a Pop-Out, the spells are not tied to the book, so they can go out into the world. They are free-range spells, which can cause problems if the Popper escapes. So let's see a Pop-Out in action."

Old Zeb pointed at the second book. Archie opened it, and there was another loud *pop*. This time something blue fluttered from the pages.

"Take this splendid dragonfly," Old Zeb said, his eyes sparkling.

Archie regarded the small blue creature that was now sitting on a bookshelf, watching him. With a shock, he realized that it was a perfectly formed miniature dragon, about five inches long, complete with tiny talons and leathery wings. At that moment it snapped its tiny jaws and snorted a jet of fire from its nostrils.

"That isn't an ordinary dragonfly, is it?"

"No," chuckled the old bookbinder. "It's called a Snap-dragon, and they can give you a nasty singe if they catch you off guard."

He held up the cover of the book, which was called *Magical Miniatures*. "There are all sorts of nasty little beasties in here."

The Snapdragon opened its wings and launched itself into the air. It made a circuit of the workshop and then tried to dive-bomb Archie, who ducked. Next it unleashed an attack on Old Zeb, who dodged out of the way just in time as it scorched the stool he had been sitting on. Then it flew through the open door and disappeared up the passageway.

"Shouldn't we try to catch it?" asked Archie.

"Oh, I don't think it will cause too much trouble," said Old Zeb. "They only last a few minutes, and it can't get past the curtain because it's enchanted."

At that moment they heard a shriek from upstairs.

"Oh dear, sounds like Marjorie has found the Snapdragon," said Old Zeb.

Archie grinned. "Or more like the Snapdragon has found Marjorie!"

The old bookbinder pulled a face like a mischievous schoolboy. "Oh dear, oh dear," he said, but he didn't seem too concerned.

"What other sorts of magical books do you know about?" he asked Archie.

Archie tried to remember what Bramble had told him. "Well, there's Drawing Books," he said.

"Yes." The old bookbinder nodded. "Jolly treacherous they are, too. Technically speaking, you know, they are magic portals—doorways that can pull you into another world—so I won't show you an actual example. Too dangerous."

Later that morning, Archie was just finishing stitching a loose leaf into a book of magical recipes called *The Culinary Cauldron: Banquets That Go with a Bang*, when Old Zeb yawned and stretched.

"We'll do one more book, and that will be enough for today. Pass me that old almanac. It should have been done days ago, but with Geoffrey still missing, we're in a bit of a muddle."

Archie recognized the Ripleys' almanac. The old bookbinder squinted at its leather cover through his magnifying glass. "*The Alchemists' Household Almanac*," he wheezed. "Dated 1603—it's over four hundred years old."

Archie thought about his book. Horace Catchpole had said it was over four hundred years old, too. Perhaps there was a connection.

"Hmm—unusual cover," mumbled Old Zeb. "Made from some sort of lizard's skin. Well, I never. It's chameleon. You don't see that very often. How interesting. Perhaps that's why it's a Special Instruction? I can see it's got a crooked spine, too. We'll have to see about that."

The old bookbinder placed the book in the book press. Then he turned a large screw handle like a wing nut until the wooden jaws of the press closed on the book. As he did, Archie heard a voice screaming.

"Help me! Please help me! The old man is cruel—he is killing me! Nooooo!"

Archie covered his ears with his hands and tried to block out the pitiful shrieks. Old Zeb turned the screw another turn, and the screaming stopped. Archie felt a mix of sadness and relief.

Old Zeb looked at him. "Whatever is the matter?"

"Didn't you hear it?" asked Archie, shocked.

"Hear what?"

Archie glanced at Old Zeb, but the old man looked unmoved. If he had heard the cries, he did not show it. What the books had told him must be true, then—no one else could hear their voices.

Old Zeb unclamped the almanac. To Archie's great relief, the book was silent.

The old man handed the almanac to Archie. "Go and ask Marjorie if we know anything else about its history." He paused and then added, "But bring the book straight back to me. That's very important. Don't let it out of your sight. And remember—"

"I know," said Archie, "third door on the right."

⌐

Archie's mind was still reeling as he made his way up the stairs. What was this strange gift that he possessed? What was he supposed to do with it? He peeked through the velvet curtain. The bookshop was empty except for Marjorie.

"The almanac you wanted Old Zeb to look at," he said, holding it up. "Do we know anything about its history?"

Marjorie peered at the book in his hand. "No," she said. "All we know is that it came from the Ripley family. But remind him it's urgent. With Greaders about, we can't take any chances. The other new arrivals are in there," she added, indicating the cardboard box where Archie had put his book, "but they can wait."

At that moment the doorbell clanged, announcing the arrival of a customer.

"Yes?" Marjorie said. "Can I help you?"

Archie stared at the almanac in his hand. Did Marjorie suspect that it was the book the Greaders were after? Was that why it was urgent? And if the almanac was in danger, was his book at risk, too?

Archie glanced at the bookcase. He hadn't heard the books whispering for several days. *The Little Book of Blessings* had said that a book whisperer could talk to magical books. Perhaps the almanac could tell him what was going on. It was worth a try.

"Hello," he whispered. "Can you hear me?"

Silence.

He tried again. "Are you all right?"

Still nothing. He shook his head. He must be mad, he thought, trying to talk to a book. He made his way back down the spiral stairs. When he reached the shadowy flagstone passageway, he heard a soft voice.

"So, *you* are the book whisperer?" it said. "How interesting."

Archie peered into the shadows. "Who's there?" he cried, his voice cracking. "Who are you?"

"You started the conversation," said the voice. It was coming from the almanac.

Archie felt the hairs on the back of his neck prickle. "What sort of book are you?" he asked, suddenly wary.

"My last master wished me to be an almanac," the voice replied slyly. "But I can be any sort of book you desire. What is your pleasure?"

Archie was taken aback.

"Er . . . I don't know," he mumbled. "I just thought you might need protecting from Greaders. . . ."

"How perceptive of you!" said the book. "But it's not just Greaders—the old bookbinder can't be trusted either. He means me harm. He didn't need to put me in that clamp. He is cruel. He's working for the Greaders."

"Old Zeb?" said Archie. "Surely not."

"The old man isn't what he seems," said the Almanac. "He has a secret he doesn't want you to know. It's behind the second door."

"You are mistaken," said Archie.

"If you don't believe me, look for yourself."

"He warned me not to open the other doors," said Archie.

"Exactly, and why do you think that is?" sneered the Almanac.

"He's trying to protect me, that's all. It's not safe," said Archie. He didn't want to believe what the Almanac was insinuating. But a seed of doubt had been sown in his mind.

The Almanac seemed to sense his unease. "Have it your own way," it said. "But don't say I didn't warn you!"

Archie stopped outside the blue door. It was the same door he had heard strange noises coming from before. He noticed something odd about the door; something missing. Then he realized that there was no door handle. He was already curious to know what was behind it, and now he was even more intrigued. He knew he should return to the Mending Workshop, but he hesitated.

Marjorie and Old Zeb had both warned him not to open any of the doors except the Mending Workshop. Now that he thought about it, that did seem suspicious. What were they keeping in there that they didn't want him to see? He was about to move on when he heard a groaning sound, like ice moving.

Archie put his ear to the door and listened.

"I told you the old man has a secret," said the Almanac.

"But what's in there?" asked Archie, still unsure whether to believe the book.

"Why don't you take a look for yourself?"

"But how can I open the door?" Archie said. "There's no door handle!"

"Surely you're not going to let a little thing like that stop you?" said the Almanac. "You're supposed to be a book whisperer, after all! The answer's there—you just need to put your finger on it."

Archie stared at the door again. What was the Almanac talking about? There was definitely no handle. Unless . . .

He reached out his hand to where the handle should have been, and to his surprise his fingers touched something solid. He closed his hand around it. There was a door handle after all! It was just invisible. The Almanac

had been right. The answer was there, in front of him.
And if the book was right about that, perhaps it was telling the truth about Old Zeb, too?

Cautiously, Archie began to turn the door handle.
Very, very slowly he put his weight against it. The door
opened a crack.

CHAPTER 20

Behind the Blue Door

A blast of cold air hit Archie's face, making him gasp. He pushed the door open a little more. Something glittered on the ground, like a myriad of tiny diamonds reflecting the light. Ice. The floor was covered with it.

The air on this side of the door was freezing, and he could see his breath hanging in the air like fog and feel it catching in his lungs. Long icicles hung from the ceiling, and somewhere nearby he could hear water dripping.

Archie squeezed through the narrow gap. His shoes made crunching sounds as they disturbed the frost-covered floor. He had not taken more than ten steps when an amber light came on. Archie stopped in his tracks.

With a shock, he realized that it wasn't a light at all but a very large eye that had just opened. Something was watching him from the darkness.

Archie's heart was thumping in his chest, and his legs felt wobbly. Then he heard it, the deep, gravelly, growling sound of some terrible beast. Archie felt the Almanac twitch in his hand.

"Run for your life!" it shrieked. "The beast is coming."

Archie turned and ran for it. Thankfully, the door was still ajar, and he could see a sliver of light. But as he raced toward it, he slipped and fell, sliding across the frosty flagstones on his stomach.

The Almanac flew out of his hand and skidded across the floor and out through the open door. The light was poor, but Archie thought he saw something moving on the surface of the book. It looked like black worms, writhing all over the cover. When he looked again, they were gone. He heard the growling sound behind him.

Convinced the awakened beast was about to pounce, Archie scrambled to his feet and bolted for the door. He twisted his body sideways and squirmed through. The door slammed shut behind him.

Archie rested his hands on his knees while he caught his breath. As his ragged breathing began to slow, he shivered. His clothes were coated in a fine layer of glistening hoarfrost, like a lawn on a winter's morning.

What sort of creature was Old Zeb keeping in there? Did the Museum Elders know about it?

Archie stared at the Almanac lying on the ground at his feet. Its cover was still and intact. Whatever he thought he'd seen must have been a trick of the light.

"What was that thing?" he demanded. But the book was silent.

⁓

When he got back to 32 Houndstooth Road that afternoon, Archie couldn't wait to tell Bramble and Thistle about the beast behind the blue door.

"What do you think it is?" he said, after recounting his close call.

"It definitely sounds like a magical beast," said Bramble. "I suppose it could be some random Popper that's escaped from the menagerie."

"The menagerie?" asked Archie, who had heard it mentioned before. "What's that?"

"The mythical menagerie is what's left of Alexander the Great's collection of magical creatures," said Bramble. "There's one or two actual creatures, but these days they are mostly Poppers. That's probably what you saw."

"I suppose so, but a Popper would ezaporate, and I think it's been there awhile," said Archie.

"But why would Old Zeb keep a magical beast under the Aisle of White?" asked Thistle. "It doesn't make any sense."

"Unless he's working for the Greaders," said Archie darkly. "He was very insistent that I was to bring the almanac straight back to him. I wonder if he means to pass it on to them."

"That's ridiculous," said Bramble, but she didn't seem completely convinced. "And anyway, what's that got to do with the beast behind the blue door?"

"I don't know," admitted Archie. "But it must be against the Lore to hoard magical creatures. And that's not all. I think the beast was protecting something."

"Why do you say that?" asked Bramble.

Archie shook his head. "I don't know. It's just a hunch. Anyway, whatever the creature is, it was asleep until I went in and disturbed it."

"What on earth possessed you to open the door in the first place?" demanded Thistle.

Archie shrugged. He couldn't tell them that the Almanac had put the idea in his head and sowed the seed of doubt about the old bookbinder. He hadn't worked out how his cousins would react to his book-whispering secret. "I was just curious," he said.

"You are a maniac!" Thistle declared. "Certifiable!"

Part of Archie was secretly pleased that his cousins thought him daring and slightly mad. But he still didn't tell them about his strange conversations with the books. It was one thing to be slightly mad—and quite another to be stark raving.

"I'll do some research in the museum," Bramble offered. "See if I can't find out what it is. Especially since you're working so close to it, Arch!"

So now they had two mysteries on their hands— solving the riddle and finding out what kind of creature Old Zeb was keeping under the Aisle of White.

"Anyway, whatever it is, you're lucky it didn't eat you or worse!" said Thistle.

"I suppose so," said Archie, wondering what could be worse than being eaten.

CHAPTER 21

The Dragon Expert

It was a few days later when things took a more sinister turn. Bramble, having made no progress with identifying the beast, was now devoting her time and energy to solving the riddle from the scroll. As her apprenticeship was in the museum itself, it didn't look suspicious if she stayed late researching. That evening, Archie had waited behind to have a hot chocolate with her at Quill's. By the time they left, it was getting dark.

"I asked around at the museum to see if any of the apprentices had any idea what you saw behind the blue door," said Bramble. "Meredith Merrydance thought it sounded like a dragon."

"No, I don't think it's a dragon," said Archie, amazed to hear himself saying such a thing. "It didn't smell like a dragon somehow."

Bramble raised her eyebrows. "And what exactly does a dragon smell like?" she asked.

"I don't really know," admitted Archie. "But I think it would have more of a stench or something. Besides, dragons breathe fire, and it was really cold."

"Now you're some kind of an expert on dragons!" exclaimed Bramble. "Is there no end to your talents?"

"Very funny," said Archie. "But I'm serious."

He told her about his father's copy of *Creatures to Avoid If You Are of a Nervous Disposition*. "There were lots of dragons in there—their eyes were red and full of cunning. But the creature I saw had amber eyes."

"So we still don't know what it is," groaned Bramble. "And I can't make head nor tail of that riddle either. I spoke to Enid Drew; she's a whiz with magical languages. Not as quick as you, of course, Arch," she teased. "Anyway, Enid said that Enochian was popular with magicians in the sixteenth and seventeenth centuries, but no one uses it anymore because it's too hard."

"So we still don't have much to go on," Archie said as they walked up the steps into the small courtyard by the

Aisle of White. "Just that mysterious symbol on the clasp of my book—the same one that's on the scroll. If only we knew who sent the riddle and the book—and if it was the same person."

"I bet we could find the symbol if we did some more research at the museum!" Bramble exclaimed excitedly, her eyes shining in the dark.

"Bram, you're already working late every night on deciphering the riddle. If anyone should be trying to find the symbol, it should be me."

"I can handle it," she said.

Archie glanced across at her. She looked tired. His cousin had more energy and enthusiasm than anyone he'd ever known, but the late nights were taking their toll. Archie let her walk a few paces ahead.

"So, what do you think?" Bramble asked casually over her shoulder. "About finding the symbol, I mean?"

Archie didn't answer. He was standing very still.

"Arch?"

"Shhhhh," he whispered. "I think there's someone there."

There was a movement in the shadows and a dark figure lunged at him, catching hold of his wrist. Archie tried to pull away, but his attacker held him tight.

"Where is the book?" it hissed in his ear. "Give it to me—if you want your cousins to live!"

"What book?" Archie stammered.

"Don't play games with me, Archie Greene. You know what book. You have no idea what you are dealing with!"

"I haven't got it."

"But you had it!" the voice accused. "Where is it now?"

His attacker loosened his grip just for a second. Archie saw his chance and yanked his arm free. "Run, Bram, run!"

His assailant lunged for him again and caught hold of Archie's sweatshirt. At that moment, a door opened across the courtyard, and someone ran up the steps with a torch.

"Hey, what's going on?" Archie recognized Pink's voice. She must have heard the commotion from Quill's.

The dark figure threw Archie to the ground and melted into the shadows.

Bramble ran to Archie's side. "You all right?" she asked.

"Yes, but let's get out of here before he comes back."

～

"So who attacked you?" Thistle asked when they were safely back on Houndstooth Road.

"I don't know," Archie said, shaking his head. "It all

happened so fast." The three cousins were sitting around the kitchen table. The house was dark except for a couple of candles. Loretta had already gone to bed. None of the children noticed that the serving hatch to the next room was slightly ajar.

"Whoever it was, he was after the book," continued Archie.

"But which book?" asked Thistle. "Your book or the almanac?"

"Good question. I thought it was the almanac, but now I'm wondering."

"But who would want your book?" said Thistle.

"Greaders," growled a low voice that made them all jump. Woodbine's head appeared through the serving hatch. "Greaders," he said again, darkly. "That's who."

Woodbine appeared at the kitchen door. He sat down heavily in one of the chairs.

"Had a scare, then, young'un?" he said to Archie.

Archie nodded. Woodbine was a reassuring presence. His uncle scratched his stubbly chin. "Something's not right," muttered Woodbine. "Is Geoffrey Screech still missing?"

"Yes." Archie nodded. "Marjorie is really worried about him. She's started sleeping in the bookshop."

Woodbine shook his head thoughtfully. "Worried about the Greaders, I expect. Your aunt Loretta hasn't slept properly since she heard about that boy being attacked. Probably best if we don't mention what happened tonight. Keep it between ourselves for now. It'll be Greaders who are behind it, all right. Trouble is, you can't tell who's working with them."

Woodbine rubbed his chin again. "Hmm," he growled. "One thing's certain: that book isn't safe where it is."

CHAPTER 22

A Midnight Excursion

Later, as the two boys were settling down for the night, Archie's mind was still racing. Woodbine had said his attacker must be a Greader, but Archie wondered how the man had known about the book. Perhaps he had overheard Bramble and him talking in Quill's. It was a warning that they should be more careful.

Woodbine had said something wasn't quite right. Perhaps he suspected someone inside the museum? Archie thought about what the Almanac had said about Old Zeb. If the old bookbinder was working for the Greaders, then none of the books at the bookshop were safe. The more Archie thought about his book sitting in a box in plain sight, the more worried he felt.

He thought about his book again. The book must be from the same person who had sent the riddle, he reasoned. Horace Catchpole had said he was a magician. But why would a magician have sent him the book? How did he even know Archie would be born in four hundred years' time? What was special about him, anyway? And then he had a sudden thought. What if the magician had sent him the book because only a book whisperer could protect it?

"Psssst, Thistle," he hissed. "Wake up. I've got to get my book."

"Yeah, yeah," said Thistle's groggy voice. "First thing in the morning."

"No," whispered Archie. "I have to get it now."

Thistle sat up and rubbed the sleep from his eyes. "You mean right now?"

Archie nodded. Thistle grinned. "A midnight raid on the Aisle of White!" he whispered. "Excellent. Shall we wake Bram?"

"No," said Archie. "She's been working late at the museum. She needs some rest. Besides, we can handle this on our own."

It was just after midnight when Archie and Thistle let themselves out of 32 Houndstooth Road. The streets of Oxford were transformed at night. The ancient sandstone buildings appeared in sepia tones like an old-fashioned photograph. Mysterious puddles of darkness lurked at every turn. The two boys cautiously made their way through the narrow cobbled lanes.

When they arrived at the bookshop, it was in darkness. A single light on in Quill's was the only illumination in the small courtyard.

"How are we going to get in?" hissed Thistle.

"I've got a key," Archie replied, producing it from his pocket. He fumbled with the lock, trying to find the keyhole.

"You know what we're doing is against the Lore, don't you?" said Thistle.

"Yes," said Archie. He was all too aware of it. "But I've got to trust my instincts on this one."

An owl hooted nearby.

"Hurry up!" urged Thistle. "Someone will see us."

Archie turned the key and pushed the door open. The bell clanged loudly, making both of them jump.

"Geoffrey, is that you?" they heard Marjorie mumbling in her sleep.

"Shhhh," whispered Archie. "I forgot about Marjorie."

They stood still, waiting to see whether she would wake up, relieved when they heard her resume snoring soundly.

Very gently, Archie closed the door behind them, leaving it on the latch so they could make a quick getaway if needed. He turned off his flashlight so that he wouldn't disturb Marjorie.

The bookshop was eerie in the dark. The aisles between the bookcases were like dark alleyways where anything or anyone could be lurking. All Archie had to do was locate the book in the cardboard box, which would only take a second. But first he had to find it.

"You stay here and keep an eye out," he whispered to Thistle. "I'll get the book."

Archie crept forward in the dark, using his hand to guide him in the gloom. Inch by inch he guided himself toward the back of the shop. He was about halfway when he heard a whispered voice.

"Who's there?" it asked urgently from behind the curtain. Archie recognized the voice of *The Little Book of Blessings.*

"It's me," he whispered. "Archie."

"Hello, Archie. I'm glad it's you." The voice sounded relieved.

"I haven't heard any of the other books whisper for days now," said Archie, keeping his voice low so that Thistle wouldn't hear. "Is everything all right?"

"Something is stealing our magic, and whatever it is is getting stronger," she said. "The other books are too scared to speak anymore." The little book sounded frightened. "Anyway, why are you sneaking around in the middle of the night? Have you come to help us?"

"Er . . . it's a long story," said Archie. "I've come to collect a book I left here."

"That book!" said *The Little Book of Blessings*. "Yes, you must take it away. It isn't safe for any magical books to be here."

Archie suddenly felt very uneasy. The bookshop seemed full of menace now. *The Little Book of Blessings* was silent.

Archie steeled himself and moved forward. His hand touched the cardboard box. He flicked on his flashlight, directing its beam down so that it wouldn't wake Marjorie, and rummaged through the box until he found what he was looking for. His fingers closed on the book, and he felt a wave of relief.

"I've got it!" he whispered, turning off the flashlight.

"Good. Now let's get out of here," Thistle whispered

back. "I think there's someone out there watching us."

Archie gazed around the bookshop at the darkness. He could hear Marjorie snoring lightly. He felt like something was watching him. He spoke again to *The Little Book of Blessings*, his voice urgent.

"Do you want me to take you, too?"

"No," she said. "Go now! Quickly! Before it is too late!"

Archie hesitated for another second. "Thanks for the warning," he whispered into the darkness.

"Bless you, Archie Greene. May you find the path that is meant for you."

Thistle was peering anxiously out into the courtyard toward Quill's. "Come on," he whispered, and they slipped out into the night.

———

When they got back to 32 Houndstooth Road, they couldn't resist waking Bramble to tell her what they had done.

"Well, you should have included me," she said crossly. "I don't see why you should have all the fun."

"Shhhh, keep your voice down, Bram," hissed Thistle. "You'll wake Mum and Dad."

"It was my fault," said Archie. "I thought you needed the rest after all the research you've been doing."

Archie put the book on the bed. It looked even more

mysterious in the glow of the flashlight.

"You were right, Archie," said Bramble, inspecting the silver clasp. "It is the same symbol as on the scroll. By the look of that scorch mark, I'd say it had been in a fire at some point, too. That could mean it was in the Great Library of Alexandria."

"So it could be good or it could be evil?" said Thistle.

"Yes," mused Bramble. "Judging by the writing on the cover, the riddle is written in Enochian script, the language of angels."

"And angels are good, right?" said Thistle.

"Well, yes," said Bramble, relaxing a bit. "I suppose so. It's weird that you could understand it, though, Archie."

Archie felt uncomfortable. "That was a fluke," he said. "I mean, how could I possibly understand a magic language that I've never seen before? Besides, I tried to read this book when I first got it and couldn't, so why was I able to read the riddle?"

"Dunno," said Thistle. "And it's not as if the book can tell us."

Archie felt the blood drain from his face. Thistle was right—ordinarily, a book couldn't speak, even a magic book, unless you were a book whisperer! Archie had a horrible sinking feeling.

His thoughts were interrupted by Thistle. "How do you open this wretched clasp?" he asked in frustration.

"You turn it like a dial," said Archie, without thinking.

"Well, I've tried that," said Thistle. "There must be some special knack to it."

"Not really," said Archie. "I just turned it until it clicked open."

"Well, be my guest," said Thistle, handing him the book.

Archie turned the clasp as he had done the first time he'd opened it. A picture of a bolt of lightning appeared in the tiny window, but it didn't open. He tried again. This time an icon of a smiling skull appeared, but still it wouldn't budge. He turned the clasp a third time, and the crystal ball appeared. Archie now knew that these symbolized the different types of magic.

"That's it," he declared, tugging at the clasp, but it remained locked tight. "Well, that's really strange," he said, his voice rising in frustration. "It opened before."

They heard footsteps on the landing.

"Uh-oh," said Thistle. "Quick, hide the book!"

Archie slipped it into his tool bag.

The door opened and the light came on.

"What on earth are you doing awake at this time?"

asked Loretta. "Isn't it bad enough that we're under attack from Greaders, without you three staying up half the night?"

She suddenly burst into tears. Woodbine appeared at her side and laid a reassuring hand on her arm.

"It's all right, Loretta," he said. "The Museum Elders won't let the Greaders get their hands on any magical books."

"But what about that poor boy, Peter Quiggley?" wailed Loretta. "Whatever is it coming to when the apprentices aren't safe to go about their business?"

Archie wondered whether his uncle had told Loretta about him being attacked outside Quill's after all. But Woodbine drew his finger across his mouth to indicate his lips remained sealed. Loretta wiped her eyes.

"Yes, well, I'm sure you're right," she sniffed. "But it's so unsettling. I mean, if the Greaders were to get hold of one of the Terrible Tomes . . . it doesn't bear thinking about."

She wiped her eyes. Then, regaining some composure, she turned to the children.

"You three. Bed. Now!"

CHAPTER 23

Break-in News

The next morning Archie and Bramble walked into Oxford as usual. They had just turned into the narrow lane that led to the Aisle of White when a police car passed them.

"I'll meet you later at Quill's," Archie began when they reached the enclosed courtyard, but his voice was drowned out by the sound of the siren. Bramble was looking at the ground.

"What's that?" she asked.

"Looks like broken glass," Archie replied.

"Hmm," agreed Bramble, gazing over his shoulder. "And that's not all. Look!"

"Oh no!" gasped Archie. "There's been a break-in at the Aisle of White!"

The area immediately outside the bookshop was cordoned off with yellow fluorescent tape. The shop window had been shattered.

Bramble flashed a look at Archie. "You and Thistle got here just in time," she gasped. Archie nodded numbly.

They crunched their way across the broken glass and peered through the open doorway into the bookshop. Several of the bookcases had been knocked flat, and books were strewn all over the floor, their spines broken. The shop sign was lying on the ground among the debris.

A low sobbing sound was coming from the far end of the shop. The two cousins picked their way through the wreckage to the curtain and peeked through.

Marjorie sat in an armchair with her head in her hands. Her face was puffy, and her tears had left her eyes red. Her hair, never her tidiest feature, was sticking up in thick clumps. She would have been a comical sight under other circumstances, but Archie and Bramble were too kind to laugh at her.

Old Zeb was trying to comfort her. Archie was relieved to see that the bookcase with *The Little Book of Blessings* and the other magic books was still standing.

"Marjorie, dear, you've had a terrible fright," soothed Old Zeb. "Have a cup of tea—you'll feel better."

"Th-th-thank you!" she sobbed, her hands rattling the cup in the saucer and spilling most of the tea. "My p-p-poor nerves! I really don't think I can take any more."

At that moment she caught sight of the children through the curtain. "It's them! It's the Greaders come back to finish me off!" she wailed.

"Sorry," said Archie. "We didn't mean to scare you. We saw the shop and came to see if you were all right."

Old Zeb put his hand on Marjorie's arm. "There, there, my dear," he said kindly. "Don't get yourself all worked up again. You're safe now."

"What happened?" Bramble asked.

Old Zeb answered, "Marjorie was asleep in the chair when someone broke in. They crept back here and tied her up in her chair while she slept."

Marjorie wiped her nose with a handkerchief. "I woke up and there he was!" she howled.

"Who?" Bramble and Archie asked at the same time.

"Him!" wailed Marjorie. "The Greader!"

"Did you get a good look at him?" Bramble asked.

Marjorie shook her head. "No, it was dark and he was wearing a cloak! He kept asking about a book," she sobbed plaintively. "Where was the special book? Where was the book that Mr. Screech was expecting?"

Bramble and Archie exchanged looks.

"It's a good thing the almanac was in the Mending Workshop, because the Greader couldn't find it. The next thing I knew, Dr. Rusp was there. Heaven knows he's not my favorite man, but I have never been so pleased to see him!"

"Rusp was passing the shop and saw the broken window," explained Old Zeb. "He must have scared the Greaders off. Just as well he did."

"What time was this?" asked Bramble.

"Oh, it must have been just after one," said Marjorie. "I heard the old grandfather clock strike the hour."

"Odd time to be walking the streets," suggested Bramble.

"Yes, I suppose it is," Old Zeb agreed. "But he's an odd fellow, Rusp."

"Did the Greaders take anything?" Archie asked.

"Nothing as far as we can tell," said Old Zeb. "Of course, it will take days to clear up the mess!" Marjorie started to howl again.

"Was anything taken from the workshop?" Bramble asked.

Old Zeb smiled. "No. People know not to go down to the workshop at night. We have some special security down there!"

Archie thought of the beast behind the blue door and gave an involuntary shiver. The old man's eyes twinkled. Archie wondered again what he was up to. Was he plotting with the Greaders, or was the beast there to stop them?

"Anyway, there'll be no bookbinding today," Old Zeb said. "Find yourself a broom, and let's get this mess cleared up."

They spent the rest of the morning picking up bookcases and sorting through the damaged books. Some were beyond repair, but most were salvageable. By midmorning a glazier had arrived to repair the window.

"You two run on home now," Old Zeb told them. "I'll look after Marjorie."

Archie and Bramble were glad to get away. They had things to discuss. They walked home as fast as they could.

"Marjorie said the break-in was just after one in the morning. That means it wasn't long after Thistle and I were there," said Archie.

"Yes," said Bramble. "Let's hope no one saw you. Bit

suspicious that it should be Rusp who came to the rescue."

"Yes," said Archie thoughtfully. "Why was he out so late?"

"Well, we know he was interested in a certain book. It could have been him who grabbed you, and when you told him you didn't have the book, he guessed it was in the bookshop."

"But why come back and raise the alarm?" asked Archie.

"Perhaps he thought he'd been seen and doubled back to cover his tracks. There's something else," Bramble added. "When I was searching through the debris, I found this. It's an Imagining Glass."

"Let me see," Archie said. He turned it over in his hand, examining it. It had a finely patterned silver handle and a rose-tinted lens.

"Hang on a minute," he said. "This is the one I saw in the museum."

"So if it was dropped by the intruder," reasoned Bramble, "then it must be someone with access to the museum."

Her eyes met Archie's.

"Rusp!"

CHAPTER 24

The Lost Books Department

When Archie arrived at the Aisle of White the next day, a man was up a ladder hanging the wooden sign back up. A note in the window said CLOSED FOR REPAIRS.

Archie let himself in, locking the door behind him. Marjorie was nowhere to be seen, and Archie guessed she was taking some time off to recover from her ordeal. He hurried down to Old Zeb's workshop.

"Ah, there you are," the old man said. "We have an urgent job to do today. There's a book that needs to go to the Lost Books Department to be classified. Should have been done sooner. Although I'm not sure it's the great book of magic they're expecting."

The old man picked up his tool bag. Archie glanced at his own tool bag, with his book hidden inside.

"Now, hurry up because we mustn't be late."

~

Old Zeb led Archie through the Great Gallery, past the Scriptorium, and through another archway, which led into a smaller gallery. A marble staircase led up to a landing on another floor. They climbed the stairs and stopped outside a set of double doors. Old Zeb knocked and they went in.

The first thing that struck Archie was how cluttered the room was. It was piled high with items of every description, mostly books and scrolls, many of them yellowing and dog-eared, but there were also paintings and sculptures, glass phials, and an assortment of curious mechanical contraptions.

At the far end, a log burned in an large, open fireplace. Leaning against it, with his back to them, was a man in a brown moleskin suit watching the flames. He was of average height and build, with dark, curly hair.

The man turned to greet them. That was when Archie noticed his eyes. They were different colors like his own: one was blue, and the other was gray. Archie had never seen anyone else with mismatched eyes. His gran had told him it was a sign of special intelligence. It ran in the family, she said, but he had wondered if it was just something she said to make him feel better when the other kids teased him.

"Come in, come in!" the man cried. "Gideon Hawke, head of Lost Books. You must be Archie."

Gideon Hawke! Bramble had told Archie that Gideon was one of the few Museum Elders to possess magical powers. Was it a coincidence that they had the same eyes?

"Now then, Zeb," he said, turning to the old bookbinder. "You're here because of the break-in at the Aisle of White?"

Old Zeb nodded. "Yes, terrible business," he said. "There's not been anything like it since the fire twelve years ago." He shook his head. "Marjorie is in a real state. She's frightened the Greaders will come back."

"And Geoffrey Screech?"

"Still missing."

"Hmm," mused Hawke, waving a hand toward a gnarled brown leather sofa next to a large desk that was overflowing with papers. "Please, sit down."

He regarded Archie with curiosity.

"In case you are wondering, our job in Lost Books is to identify magical books that have gone astray. When a new book arrives, it comes here to be classified according to its magical strength. I understand that you have a book with a Special Instruction. Can I see it?"

Archie felt his face redden. Hawke was looking straight at him. He must know he'd taken the book! This was a disaster. Archie had broken the Lore, and now he had been found out. There was nothing for it but to admit his guilt and face the consequences. His would be the shortest-lived apprenticeship in the history of the museum. He would leave in disgrace.

Archie glanced at his tool bag, where the book was hidden. He was just about to confess what he'd done when Old Zeb said, "He hasn't got it. I have." The old bookbinder produced the almanac from his own battered tool bag and placed it on the desk. Archie breathed a huge sigh of relief.

Hawke slowly approached the book. He reached out one hand toward it.

"The magic doesn't seem particularly strong," he said, raising his eyebrows. "I wonder why it's a Special Instruction."

Hawke opened a drawer and took out an Imagining Glass with a black handle. It had a motif of an eye etched into it, and instead of clear glass, the lens was tinted a silvery gray. He inspected the book's cover minutely, moving the gray lens closer and farther away.

He caught Old Zeb's eye. "Mildly mischievous, perhaps, but I can't see anything more than that," he said. "But I have asked Morag Pandrama and Wolfus Bone to join us and to bring their classifying tools."

Just then, there was a knock on the door. A severe-looking woman with olive skin and large, almond-shaped brown eyes entered the room. She had a pince-nez perched on the end of her aquiline nose and a quill pen pushed into her hair. In her arms she carried a pile of ancient books.

"I have brought the indexes from the Great Library," she said.

"Morag is the museum's archivist," Hawke kindly explained to Archie. "She will tell us if there is any mention of the book in the old records."

Morag Pandrama stacked the books she had brought with her on the floor and immediately set to work thumbing through one particularly dusty volume. Every few pages she paused to glance at the almanac, and to make occasional tutting noises through her teeth.

There was another knock on the door. The man who entered was the thinnest, gauntest man Archie had ever seen. He was so tall that he had to duck his head to fit through Hawke's door. This combined with his frail limbs made him look like a giant stick insect. The skin on his face and his close-cropped blond scalp was pulled so tight that it barely seemed to cover his skull. In one limp hand, he held what looked like a forked stick, but Archie guessed it was a dowsing rod because he'd seen pictures of people using something similar to find water.

Archie knew before Hawke introduced him that the scary-looking man must be Wolfus Bone. His large mouth was crowded with teeth, with two pronounced canines. There was something watchful about him that put Archie in mind of a predator.

"You have something for me, Gideon?" the man asked in a thick accent that sounded eastern European.

"Yes, a Special Instruction," said Hawke. "Wolfus is our master magic diviner," he added, for Archie's benefit. "He will tell us just how strong the magic is."

The two newcomers barely seemed to notice Archie; their attention was focused on the almanac on Gideon Hawke's desk. While Morag Pandrama continued to trawl through the old records, Wolfus Bone stood motionless in the center of the room, his eyes fixed on the book.

Archie gazed around at the curious objects in Hawke's study. His eyes were drawn to what looked like a black letter opener on the desk. It had a beautifully engraved handle and a blade like a black mirror, which caught the dancing firelight, reflecting sparkling shards of brilliance.

Hawke smiled. "I see you are admiring the Shadow Blade. It is made from obsidian, the black glass forged in the heat of a volcano."

Archie was fascinated by the play of light upon the blade. "Why does it sparkle like that?"

"It is the reflection of a shooting star captured in the glass."

Archie reached out to touch the blade, but Hawke caught his hand.

"Best not to touch," he warned. "It is an enchanted blade, and it has special properties. It can penetrate any darkness—and the darkest of hearts."

Archie felt a chill run down his spine. He wondered why Gideon Hawke was telling him this. Was he trying to impress him or scare him?

"What about that?" Archie asked, indicating a gnarled wooden staff with a hook at one end that was mounted on the wall above the fireplace.

"That is a Book Hook," said Hawke. "Used by the old magic writers, it can force magic back into a book, or extract something that is trapped within. It can also destroy spells that won't obey it."

"I am ready to test the book now, Gideon," Wolfus Bone interrupted.

"Very well, Wolfus," Hawke replied. "Archie, please stand back."

Archie's attention shifted to the magic diviner. Wolfus Bone gently held the dowsing rod in his fingers and approached the book on the desk. Very, very slowly, he moved toward the book. The rod twitched in his hand.

"Hmm," said Bone. "On the surface it appears to be a moderately charmed almanac, the sort of thing any alchemist or magician might have around the house. But it is not quite what it seems. The book is deceptive. It has a concealment charm on it."

"What would be the purpose of such a charm?" asked Hawke.

"To imitate other books, in order to win the trust of their users, perhaps," said Bone.

Hawke nodded. "Or to frighten them?"

"Yes, possibly," said Bone.

Wolfus Bone suddenly grasped the Shadow Blade and held it over the almanac in a menacing way. Archie heard the book give a shriek, and its cover writhed with black worms. He stepped back in alarm.

"Did you see that?" Archie gasped. "The black worms all over the cover?"

Wolfus Bone chuckled under his breath. "Yes," he said. "Black bookworms. When it is threatened, the book is bewitched to imitate a book of dark magic. Ingenious, but a harmless trick. This is not a book to be trusted."

Archie regarded the book suspiciously. He glanced at Old Zeb. The almanac had made him doubt the old bookbinder. Now he could see that it had deliberately tried to turn him against the old man. He had been naive to be taken in.

"Morag?" Hawke inquired, turning to the archivist.

She tutted. "I cannot find any record of this book in the Archive."

"Hmm," said Hawke. "So how can we classify it, then? Is it dangerous?"

"I don't know, Gideon," Bone replied, his eyes roving around the room. "I can feel a very strong magical energy, but I'm not sure where it's coming from."

The magic diviner's nose twitched. His eyes fell on Archie's tool bag. Archie pulled it closer.

Archie felt Hawke's eyes on him. "Any ideas, Archie?"

Archie felt his face color again. He wanted to come clean about the book hidden in his bag, but he was in so deep now that he couldn't see how he could explain it without getting himself and his cousins into a lot of trouble.

Hawke was watching him closely. He spoke slowly, his eyes boring into Archie's head. "When a book has a Special Instruction, it usually means that it is very powerful and possibly dangerous. The best place for a book like that is here in Lost Books. So if you come across anything of that nature, Archie, you must come and tell me. Do you understand?"

Archie nodded, avoiding eye contact.

Old Zeb pointed at the almanac. "What do you want to do with this?" he asked.

"I think we'll keep it here," Hawke said, "where it can't cause any more mischief."

⌣

When Archie and Old Zeb had gone, Wolfus Bone and Morag Pandrama remained behind. Bone warmed himself by the fire. After a while he spoke.

"Gideon, what's going on?"

Hawke raised one eyebrow. "We thought the almanac was the reason for the break-in at the Aisle of White."

Wolfus Bone snorted. "The almanac may be deceitful, but it is no more than that. But . . ."

"Yes, Wolfus?"

Bone shook his head. "I could sense something else in the room. I am certain the boy had a book concealed on him. A very special book."

"Yes, I wondered about that," said Hawke.

"Did you notice the boy's eyes?" asked Morag Pandrama. "The clearest example of Magician's Eye I've ever seen. Even more pronounced than yours."

Hawke nodded. "Yes, of course I noticed. How could I miss them?"

"What do you intend to do, Gideon?"

"For now, nothing. If Archie is breaking the Lore to hold on to a book, I want to know why. I'm going to watch him closely. Let's keep this among ourselves until we know more."

"What about the almanac?" asked Morag Pandrama.

"A decoy?" said Bone.

"Yes," said Hawke. "I think we can be sure it's not the almanac that's brought the Greaders to Oxford."

CHAPTER 25

Echoes of the Past

The Mending Workshop was quiet. Old Zeb had promised to call in on Marjorie on his way home to make sure she was all right and had left Archie to lock up. Archie turned the day's events over in his mind. He thought about his strange meeting with the Lost Books Department. He was sure that Gideon Hawke and Wolfus Bone suspected something. Had they guessed he was hiding a book?

Archie suddenly felt very alone. He desperately wanted to tell his cousins that he was a book whisperer, but he wasn't sure how they'd react. Would they think he was imagining it or making it up? If only he had some proof.

He took out his book and put it on the bench. The odd thing was that although he had heard the other magical books whisper, he had never heard his book speak. He wondered why. If the magician had sent it to him because of his special talent, this seemed strange.

"Hello," he said. "Can you hear me?"

There was no reply.

"If I'm supposed to be a book whisperer, why can't I talk to you?"

Silence.

"Look, if you don't talk to me, then I'm going to hand you in to Gideon Hawke in Lost Books first thing in the morning, which is probably what I should have done in the first place."

Still there was no reply.

"That's settled then." Archie turned away to put out the lights. But just as he did, he heard a gentle voice.

"Hello, Archie," it said. "I am so glad you came to get me. I was really frightened."

Archie stopped in his tracks. "Who are you?"

"That's not important at the moment," said the voice. "All you need to know is that there are people who want my power, and who will go to any lengths to get it. But they must never have it. You are the only one I can trust."

"But why me?" asked Archie.

"Because you have the gift. You are a book whisperer, and only a book whisperer can save me."

"But there are others in the museum with magical powers—Gideon Hawke, for one, and Wolfus Bone," protested Archie. "Can't they help you?"

"No! Hawke and Bone can't be trusted. They desire my power for themselves."

Archie's eyes narrowed. The Almanac had tried to turn him against Old Zeb, and that had been a lie. Was this book any more trustworthy?

"What is this power you speak of?" Archie asked.

"It is the power that your father was afraid of. But it is nothing to fear. It is the power you were born to wield. It is your destiny."

"What destiny? What am I supposed to do?"

"You will understand when the time comes."

"What do you want from me?" Archie demanded.

Silence.

Archie stared at the book. It was still and quiet, but he hadn't imagined that voice. Maybe it was time to tell his cousins his secret after all. He didn't think he could carry it on his own any longer.

Bramble and Thistle were waiting for him outside Quill's. They'd decided to stick together while Archie was carrying the book, just in case there was any trouble.

As they walked home, it all came pouring out.

"I should have told you before," said Archie guiltily, "but I didn't know how."

"A book whisperer!" exclaimed Thistle, his eyes wide with wonder.

Archie felt awkward. "Yes, I know it sounds ridiculous."

"But book whispering is so cool!" said Thistle. "I mean, no one's been able to do that for centuries!"

Archie shrugged. "I think it is why the magician sent me the book."

"But how could he have known that you'd turn out to be a book whisperer?" asked Bramble. "It was four hundred years before you were even born."

"I know, it sounds crazy," admitted Archie. "But somehow he knew and sent me the book to protect. He was a magician, after all. Anyway, I thought I was protecting it from Greaders, but now it has warned me not to trust Hawke and Bone. Do you think there could be something sinister going on inside the museum?"

"Maybe that's what Dad was hinting at the other

night," said Bramble.

"Hang on, though," said Thistle. "If the magician sent you the book because you are a book whisperer, then perhaps there's something you're supposed to do with it that only a book whisperer can do."

Archie felt a sinking feeling in his stomach. "Like what?"

Thistle shrugged. "I don't know. That's what we have to find out. But whatever it is, you're not on your own, Arch. Bramble and I will help you with it."

Archie gave a thin smile. With his two cousins beside him, he didn't feel so daunted.

"And while we're sharing secrets," Thistle continued, "I've got one for you.

"I did some digging around about that almanac. We know it came from the Ripleys, so I asked Dad—he knows all about the old Flame-Keeping families. Apparently, there are rumors that the Ripleys have been hoarding magic books for years. And there are rumors that they are up to their old tricks again. Their family home is at Ripley Hall in Cornwall. They have a private library there—all very hush-hush."

"But I thought hoarding magic books was against the Lore," said Archie, making a mental note to look up

Arthur Ripley in the reference book about collectors.

"It is," said Bramble. "Keeping magic books that haven't been classified is a form of Greading."

"Exactly," said Thistle. "But Dad says no one can prove it. And there's something else. When Arthur Ripley was head of Lost Books, he had an assistant."

"I never heard that before!" said Bramble.

"Well, no, you wouldn't have," said Thistle. "You see, Arthur Ripley's assistant was Alex Greene—Archie's dad."

"What?" gasped Archie, shocked. He felt his stomach twist.

"After he was apprenticed to Old Zeb, Alex went to work with Ripley," Thistle continued. "But he left under a cloud. Dad didn't want to talk about it, but there were rumors that he was working closely with Ripley."

Archie's stomach lurched again. He felt sick. Just as he thought he knew who his father was again, he felt like the rug was being pulled from under him. "Oh, that's great," he said. "So my dad was working with Arthur Ripley when he tried to steal the Terrible Tomes and set fire to the museum!"

"Hold on," said Bramble. "We don't know what really happened. Your dad's not here to tell his side of the story, so I think we should give him the benefit of the doubt. And if he was there, then I'm sure he had a good reason."

"And talking about people getting into the Crypt, that reminds me. Vincent von Herring has called an emergency meeting. Apparently, the Museum Elders are so worried about the break-in at the Aisle of White that they are beefing up security at Mothballs. All apprentices have to attend."

~

Later, when he went to bed, Archie was still thinking about what Thistle had said about his father. It bothered him. Had Alex Greene been involved in starting the fire in the museum twelve years earlier?

He took out the shoe box with his father's things and rummaged through it until he found the photograph of Alex and Loretta. He inspected it minutely. Quill's had hardly changed at all. His father and Loretta looked so happy. He wondered what had caused the rift between brother and sister that had kept him away from his cousins for so many years.

Archie picked up the scrapbook and flicked though the pages. There were some faded photographs and newspaper cuttings. The last entry was a photograph of a baby in a carriage. "Archie aged six weeks," said a handwritten caption underneath. He turned the page, and as he did, a sheet of paper fell out.

It was a letter dated July 26, 2003—the day Archie was born. It was from Loretta to his father.

Dearest Alex,

    Congratulations on the birth of your beautiful baby boy! I know that you will be a wonderful father to him and his sister.

    You must be feeling many emotions today— great joy and great apprehension. I know that you consulted the Books of Destiny and that they did not tell you what you hoped for. But the future is shaped by what we do today as much as by the past.

    Archie is just a baby at the moment. I know that you will do whatever you can to protect him. I understand your desire to keep him away from magic, but I beg you to let him take his place at the museum. He needs to understand our world—the world that he was born into. And he needs his family. Please don't hide him away.

               Your loving sister,

               Loretta

Archie slipped the note back into the book and closed it. He did not understand it completely, but it was clear that his father had discovered something about his new-born son that troubled him. What had alarmed his dad enough that he decided to keep Archie away from the world of magic?

Archie examined the black-and-white photograph of Alex and Loretta again. Loretta had said Archie resembled his father. He looked closely at the photograph. He could see the likeness. He wondered if his father had had different-colored eyes just like him. Among the Flame Keepers, mismatched eyes were seen as a sign that someone was born with magical powers—or touched with magic. Was his father touched with magic? Had Alex Greene been a book whisperer, too? Was that his secret?

And then Archie had another thought. What if being a book whisperer had made his father do terrible things? He had been Arthur Ripley's apprentice, after all. Perhaps he'd had something to do with Ripley's plot to steal the Terrible Tomes. If so, his father might have been tormented with guilt. And then to cap it all, his son was born with mismatched eyes. He would have known that he was also likely to be a book whisperer. That might have been what spooked him. Or was there some other secret that his father knew?

Whatever it was, Archie had to know. And he had an idea how he might find out.

CHAPTER 26

The Book of Yore

At Quill's the next day, Pink was checking Firemarks. She glanced at Archie's hand before making him a Motion Potion.

"Orders from the Museum Elders," she said. "Can't be too careful with Greaders about."

Archie nodded. When he arrived at the Great Gallery, he found the place subdued. The apprentices were going about their usual tasks, but there was none of the chatter and high jinks that normally accompanied their work. It was as if all the fun had been sucked out of the place. The break-in at the Aisle of White was weighing heavily on people's minds. If the bookshop wasn't safe, then where was?

As Archie passed a group of apprentices, he overheard a whispered conversation.

"My parents say that the Greaders are getting bolder," confided a boy who Archie didn't recognize. "They say that if there's any more trouble, then they will keep me at home."

"My mum says that the museum will be next," said Meredith Merrydance. "The Greaders won't stop until they find whatever book they're after. She says it's the worst she can remember."

"That's the least of it," announced Enid Drew. "My dad says that if this Greader plot succeeds, then Mothballs will be finished."

"Well, I heard that Professor von Herring is going to close the museum and send all the apprentices home because it's too dangerous," said Meredith. "Apparently, that's what the meeting is about."

Archie hurried on. Glancing quickly around to make sure he was unobserved, he opened one of the double doors and slipped into the Scriptorium. As he stepped inside, the torches on the walls ignited, lighting the room.

Archie saw the glass dome at the far end containing the Books of Destiny. But it wasn't the future that interested him. It was the past. Bramble had said that the past was best left alone, but he had to know what had happened when he was born. He needed to know why his parents had felt it necessary to keep him away from the museum.

He turned to *The Book of Yore* and spoke to it in what he hoped was a clear, commanding voice.

"What frightened my parents when I was born?"

The book was silent and still, its dark-brown cover firmly closed.

Archie tried again. "Why didn't they tell me about the magical books?" he demanded.

The book remained closed, but Archie heard something—a voice so quiet that he might have imagined it. Like the wind blowing through the brittle branches of an ancient, long-dead tree, it sounded as old as time itself.

"The past is gone," the voice rasped. "Those who disturb it cannot change it, but they may be changed by it."

Archie knew it was a warning, but his need to know spurred him on.

"That is a chance I have to take," he declared, hoping he sounded braver than he felt.

"Very well."

The Book of Yore suddenly flipped open. Its pages turned as if some unseen hand riffled through them. Just as suddenly as it had started, it stopped, and slammed shut again. The book was still, but a bookmark had appeared in its pages.

"What is shown to the curious is not always what they hoped for," rasped the voice. "*The Book of Yore* reveals what they need to know, not what they wish to know. Your page is marked. I ask you again, do you choose to consult the past?"

"Yes, I do," said Archie.

"So be it!"

Archie stepped forward and opened the book to the page with the bookmark.

A date was written in neat copperplate script. Archie had expected it to be his birthday, but *The Book of Yore* had opened to a date four hundred years earlier, March 15, 1603.

Archie traced the date with his finger, and as he did, the surface of the book rippled as if he was disturbing the surface of a pond. His finger disappeared into the book, followed by his hand. He felt a cold sensation working up his arm. He tried to resist, but the force was too strong. By now his arm had disappeared up to the elbow, and still he was being pulled.

Archie tried to wrench his arm free, but his other hand touched the page and disappeared. The tug was too great for him to resist. He closed his eyes. Too late, he realized what sort of book *The Book of Yore* was—a Drawing Book! There was a rushing sound in his ears like wind, and he was sucked into the pages. He felt himself falling.

When he opened his eyes again, he was in a dark, book-lined room. A candle guttered, and in the flickering light he could see an old man with a long white beard and a black skullcap sitting at a table. He was staring at a crystal pendant in his hand, deep in concentration. Archie recognized the symbol engraved on the pendant.

Sitting across the table from the old man was a younger man. He had his back to Archie, so he could not see his face.

"You promised to bring me the book written in the language of angels," the old man said.

"And here it is," the younger man said, sliding a book toward him. It was the same book that Horace Catchpole had delivered to Archie.

The old man rubbed his hands together. "At last!" he cried. "I will be able to speak with the angels!"

The old man's hands grasped the book, but the younger man pulled it back. "We had an agreement," he declared.

The old man looked up. "And I have kept my part of the bargain," he said. "I used my scrying skills to discover the book whisperer as you asked. I have his name, even though he will not be born for another four hundred years."

He reached for the book again. The other man still held it back.

"The book whisperer's name?"

The old man looked at him imploringly. "I cannot tell you that. It goes against the natural Lores of Magic," he protested.

"I do not care about the Lores of Magic!" scoffed the younger man. "If you want the book, you will give me his name."

The old man hesitated, torn between desire and duty. Desire won.

"Archie Greene."

The room went dark. Archie felt himself falling again and closed his eyes. When he opened them, he was back in the Scriptorium, and *The Book of Yore* was firmly closed.

CHAPTER 27

Glyph Hanger

Archie found it hard to concentrate for the rest of the day. His thoughts were on what he'd seen in *The Book of Yore*. He was so distracted that he forgot to put any water in the kettle so that it boiled dry, and then he nearly put a magical book in the furnace instead of a log. In the end, Old Zeb sent him home early.

"I don't know what's gotten into you," the old bookbinder said. "See you tomorrow—and remember to bring your head with you," he added, shaking his own in disbelief.

For the rest of the evening, Archie could think about nothing else. He must have been sent the book because he was a book whisperer. But what he was meant to do with it and why it had frightened his father so much still a mystery.

Loretta's note to her brother said that Alex Greene had looked into one of the Books of Destiny, but it didn't say which one. Could Archie's father have consulted *The Book of Yore*? If so, had he been shown the same thing as Archie? And if he had, why had this caused him to keep his son away from the museum and his cousins?

Another thought occurred to him. What if his father had not consulted the past at all: what if he had looked into one of the other Books of Destiny and seen the future? Could Alex Greene have foreseen some terrible event that hadn't happened yet and tried to change the path his son was on? Whatever it was that Alex Greene had seen, it had alarmed him enough to keep his son away from magic. Archie knew he might be in danger, but he didn't know how.

That night, he dreamed that he was trapped inside a glass cage that was filling up with sand. He was inside the hourglass on the spine of *The Book of Reckoning* and could not get out. He woke in a cold sweat, relieved to find he was safely tucked up in the bedroom he shared with Thistle.

"Right," said Old Zeb the next day, taking a mended reference book from the clamp. "Put this back on the shelf. I'm just popping up to make sure Marjorie is all right."

Marjorie had not been the same since the break-in. Old Zeb said her nerves were bad. In fact, everyone involved with the museum seemed to have gotten the jitters.

As Archie replaced the book, he noticed *Magic Collectors Past & Present* on the same shelf. It reminded him that he had been meaning to look up Arthur Ripley. He took the book down and skimmed through the pages. The first name he came to was Alexander the Great.

Probably the most famous of all the magic collectors, Alexander sought out magical texts and instruments from the territories he conquered. . . .

A line drawing of Alexander showed a fair-haired young warrior. Archie turned the page. A very different face confronted him. It was angular with hollow cheeks, a hooked nose, and dull black eyes. Archie read the entry.

A collector of dark magic, Barzak was the most feared dark warlock of his time and was responsible for causing the magical conflagration that burned down the Great Library of Alexandria.

Archie shivered. "Well, I certainly wouldn't want to meet him on a dark night!" he muttered to himself.

He looked at the index and ran his finger down the list of names. There were several Ripleys, including a Morton Ripley and a George Ripley. But it was Arthur Ripley he wanted to know about. He turned to the entry.

The face that stared back at him bore a striking resemblance to Arabella. Arthur Ripley had the same cold gray eyes.

Among the most infamous modern collectors was the English book antiquarian Arthur Ripley. Ripley used his position as Head of Lost Books at the Museum of Magical Miscellany in Oxford to search for the Terrible Tomes, the seven most dangerous books ever written. Ripley is believed to have died in a fire at the museum, although his body was never recovered. This has led to persistent but completely unsubstantiated rumors that Ripley is still alive.

There was no mention of his assistant Alex Greene. Archie turned the page and was about to close the book when something else caught his eye.

He felt his heart skip a beat. There it was—the mysterious symbol! The same one he'd seen on the crystal pendant.

Beneath the symbol was a short explanation: *The glyph or symbol designed by John Dee to express the mystical unity of all creation.*

Next to it was a portrait of an old man with sparkling blue eyes and a long beard of purest white. He wore a black skullcap and a large white ruff around his neck in the Elizabethan style. Hanging from a silver chain around his neck was a diamond-shaped pendant made from green crystal. He was the old man who Archie had seen in *The Book of Yore.*

Below the portrait was a brief description of his life.

JOHN DEE (1527–1609). Dee was an English mathematician, astronomer, astrologer, alchemist, and navigator. One of the most learned men of his age, Dee was Queen Elizabeth I's court magician.

Magician! Archie read on.

Dee amassed one of the largest private libraries in Europe, including many rare and magical books. He dedicated his collection to Queen Elizabeth, whom Dee referred to affectionately as Gloriana.

Dee was famous for his use of crystal balls and other scrying instruments to see into the future. Several of his crystal balls are now displayed in the British Museum, but his favorite scrying crystal, the Emerald Eye, has never been found. Dee spent the latter part of his life trying to find a legendary book from the Great Library of Alexandria, which he believed would allow him to speak to angels. His association with Greaders tarnished his reputation within the magical community, and he died penniless.

"I've found the magician!" Archie announced to his cousins later. "His name is John Dee, and he was Elizabeth I's court magician. He collected magic books. But he was also fascinated by their power. It is his symbol on the clasp and on the scroll, so he must be the one who sent me the book."

"But we still don't know what he wanted you to do with it," Thistle replied, "or how you should use your book-whispering powers."

"I know," Archie said. "But we're a lot closer to finding out. The riddle holds the key, I'm sure of it."

CHAPTER 28

Under Attack

When the emergency meeting took place the next evening at Quill's, the room was full of worried faces. The apprentices were talking among themselves in whispered voices.

Gideon Hawke, Wolfus Bone, and some of the other Museum Elders were seated at the back of the room. Archie thought he recognized a short man with a goatee wearing a tweed suit. He was sitting with a gray-haired woman.

"That man next to Hawke," Archie whispered to Bramble. "I think he was in the book Old Zeb showed me . . . ?"

"Yes, that's Dr. Motley Brown," confirmed Bramble, "head of Natural Magic. And he's talking to Feodora Graves, head of Supernatural Magic."

Vincent von Herring strode onto the raised stage. He held up his hand for silence.

"Good evening, apprentices," he said with a curt nod. "I do not wish to alarm you again, but we have some important information to tell you."

He glanced across at the other Elders. Their faces were grim. Von Herring took a deep breath.

"We believe that the museum is under attack," he said.

There were horrified gasps from around the room. Von Herring continued, "You are aware of the break-in at the Aisle of White. We believe that something or someone is also stealing magic from the museum. We must assume that the enemy has found a way to infiltrate our defenses."

There were more gasps around the room as the apprentices contemplated the magnitude of what they had just heard. Trouble outside the museum was one thing, but if the Greaders had found a way inside its protected walls, that was far more worrying. When the murmuring had died down, von Herring spoke again.

"If Greaders have breached the museum's security, then no one is safe. As the head of Dangerous Books, I have called a special meeting of the Elders to decide what is to be done. Until then no apprentices are to enter the museum on their own. You must have someone with you at all times.

"We are also stepping up security in the Crypt. I don't need to tell you how dangerous it would be if someone were to open one of the Terrible Tomes and release its dark magic. The consequences could be catastrophic.

"The four Terrible Tomes that we have recovered are safely under lock and key inside the Crypt, which is located in the Lost Books Department, the most secure part of the museum. No apprentices are allowed inside the Crypt. Only the Museum Elders have keys to open it.

"Each of the Tomes is locked inside an iron cage that has enough charms and enchantments on it to keep out an army of Greaders."

There was more murmuring among the apprentices. Vincent von Herring raised his voice.

"We are doing everything possible to defend the museum from the current attack," he continued. "Rest assured, we will prevail.

"Now, I would ask you all to return to your duties. Continue as normal and report anything suspicious. Thank you, ladies and gentlemen."

There was a nervous buzz as they filed out of the meeting. Bramble and Archie ordered a couple of hot chocolates to cheer themselves up and sat down in two battered armchairs that weren't Seats of Learning. Quill's was emptying as people drifted off home.

"Do you think they will come up with a plan to defend the museum?" Archie asked.

"They'll think of something," murmured Bramble. "They always do."

Archie felt a bit better. "Well, I hope they come up with something soon," he said. "The books in the Aisle of White are really frightened. I haven't heard a peep out of them in days. I wonder if I should tell von Herring about being a book whisperer. But it might just make him suspicious."

Bramble was staring over Archie's shoulder. She spoke in a whisper. "Talking about suspicious . . . ," she said.

"Who?" asked Archie.

"Him!"

Archie looked up to see Aurelius Rusp talking to Pink.

"I'll take a Werewolf's Revenge in the Dragon's Claw," he barked.

"He's going to the museum," Bramble whispered.

"I wonder what for," Archie said.

"There's only one way to find out!" said Bramble. "Come on!"

"But you heard von Herring. We're not allowed in the museum on our own," said Archie.

"We won't be on our own." Bramble smiled. "We'll be with Rusp."

Archie was about to protest again, but at that moment Pink moved through the Permission Wall to serve a customer at the front of house, and Bramble sprang out of her chair.

"Quick," she cried, "this is our chance. You keep an eye out while I mix us a Motion Potion."

She hopped up onto the bar, swung her legs over, and slid down the other side. Then she took down two mugs and poured a couple of crimson drops from the dark-red bottle.

"Are you sure you know what you're doing?" whispered Archie. He cast an anxious glance around the room in case anyone was watching. "I mean, that's pretty advanced stuff."

"Shhhh, I've seen Pink do it loads of times," Bramble hissed over her shoulder. She took down the blue bottle and poured a tiny drop of the clear liquid into each mug.

Finally, she took down the big black bottle and added a dash. A cackling sound and a thick white cloud like mist came from the contents of the mugs.

"Told you." She smiled. "Fruit shot or a choc-tail?"

"Er . . . choc-tail," said Archie. "Just hurry up!"

Bramble pulled on the porcelain handle and topped up the mugs with steaming dark chocolate.

"There," she said, handing Archie his Motion Potion.

She had barely swung her legs back over the bar when Pink came bustling back through the Permission Wall.

"Hey, what are you two looking so pleased about?" said Pink.

"Er, nothing," said Bramble, smiling sweetly but looking slightly shifty.

The two children moved away from the bar, nursing their drinks. Archie held his book bag over his shoulder.

"I can't see Rusp anywhere," he said, scanning the room. The place was virtually deserted now. "He must have gone already."

"Yes, and we'd better get a move on, too," said Bramble. She pulled back the curtain to the Box Seats.

Archie fastened his seat belt. He eyed his mug uncertainly. "Are you sure about this?" he said. "You said that the Seats of Learning can be unstable unless you have the right Motion Potion."

Bramble smiled. "What can possibly go wrong?"

She chinked her mug against Archie's.

"Bottoms up!" She grinned.

CHAPTER 29

Crying Wolf

A particularly bumpy flight on the Box Seats later, the two cousins were standing in the Great Gallery. There was no sign of Rusp. Archie was still feeling nauseous from the ride and decided that hot chocolate and the Box Seats really didn't mix, especially with amateurs mixing the Motion Potions.

He was about to mention this to Bramble when there was a loud crash like a large piece of furniture being thrown against a wall. It was followed by the sound of splintering wood, and a rushing noise like flames racing up a chimney.

Suddenly there was a blood-chilling howl.

"It's coming from the dark magic section in the West Gallery!" Bramble cried.

They heard another howl, rising to the high, wavering, full-throated cry of a wild animal, ending in a low snarl. Another crash and the sound of more splintering wood.

"Whatever it is, it's heading this way!" Bramble exclaimed.

"We have to try to stop it before it does any more damage!" cried Archie.

He was already racing toward the sound. Bramble took a deep breath and dashed after him. They ran up a marble staircase and turned into a corridor that connected the West Gallery to the rest of the museum.

As they turned the corner, they saw an enormous wolflike creature, as tall as a small pony, with gleaming yellow eyes and shaggy gray fur. Its pointed ears looked like horns, and fire belched from its large round nostrils.

Around it was devastation. Several bookcases had been smashed to the ground. There were small pockets of fire burning around the room, and several books had been turned into charcoal and ash.

"What is that thing?" shrieked Bramble.

"It's a flarewolf!" Archie yelled back. "I saw a picture of one in that reference book. Part dragon, part wolf. Very nasty."

"It must be a Pop-Out!" Bramble exclaimed.

The flarewolf was scanning the room with its gleaming eyes. It threw back its head and howled again. Two flares shot from its nostrils like a flamethrower, setting fire to a large oriental tapestry on the wall.

"Why isn't it ezaporating?" Bramble called, moving closer to her cousin.

"I don't know, but I think we should RUN!" shouted Archie.

At that moment the flarewolf heard them. Its large head whipped around, and it fixed the two cousins with its glittering yellow eyes. Archie felt the fear well up inside him.

"Did I mention run?" he cried again, as they darted back in the direction they had just come.

Bramble sprinted back along the corridor and up another staircase toward the Lost Books Department. Archie raced after her. The creature howled again, and Archie felt a rush of searing hot air ruffle his hair. The two cousins ducked around the corner as the flarewolf's flaming breath hit the wall behind them.

The flarewolf had followed them and was now watching them from less than ten feet away.

"Quick, open that door," Bramble cried.

Archie tried to open the door, but it was locked.

"We're cornered," he said. "Now what?"

The flarewolf was stalking them. Its mouth was open, and long strands of drool dripped onto the floor.

Bramble was staring at the beast. "I just don't understand how it escaped," she said. "I mean, who would let something like that out?"

The flarewolf fixed her with its yellow eyes. In its head it could hear a voice. "Kill the girl!" it said. The flarewolf did not know where the voice was coming from, only that it must obey. It crouched low on its haunches, snarling.

"Now what?" gasped Archie.

"I'll think of something," said Bramble.

"Good," said Archie, "but can you hurry up? I don't think wishful thinking is going to keep us safe."

"Keep us safe!" cried Bramble. "Brilliant, Archie. My Keep Safe!"

She slipped off her bracelet and grasped the tiny

golden bow in her hand. With her left arm straight, she drew back an imaginary bowstring.

The flarewolf wrinkled its large muzzle in a snarl and advanced toward them. Archie took a step backward and realized he was up against the wall with nowhere else to go. At that moment, Bramble released her right hand. To Archie's amazement, a tiny golden arrow arced through the air and buried itself in the flarewolf's leg. The creature howled with pain and ripped at the arrow with its teeth.

"That really was brilliant!" cried Archie. "Now, run!"

They took off again as fast as they could, racing down a flight of marble stairs to the East Gallery. The flarewolf threw back its head and howled, sending jets of flame into the air. They could hear it leaving a trail of destruction as it gave pursuit.

"Quick, in here!" cried Bramble, opening a door off the gallery.

The two cousins ducked through into a dark corridor, and Bramble slammed the door behind them.

There was a scratching sound on the other side of the door, then another long howl, and they heard the flarewolf direct its flames at the door. The wood crackled and the handle glowed red hot.

"It won't take it long to burn its way through," said Archie. "Where are we?"

"This corridor leads to the Archive."

"Is there another way out?"

Bramble shook her head. "No, the Archive is next to the Crypt, which is always kept locked. You heard von Herring—only the Museum Elders have keys. There is supposed to be a secret entrance to the Crypt, but it's not from inside the museum, and it's guarded night and day. The only other way out of here is back the way we came."

Archie glanced at his cousin. Her hair was smoking and her face was smudged with soot smuts. She looked pale and shaken, but she was putting a brave face on it.

"I guess we're trapped then," Archie whispered.

~

On the other side of the door, the flarewolf heard the voice again inside its dark heart. It was the same voice that had released it and told it to find the children.

"Kill the girl but bring the boy!" the voice commanded. "Archie Greene must live!"

The beast gave a low growl. One more blast from its

flames and the door would give way. It was about to flare again when its sensitive ears heard something behind it. Human voices.

"What on earth . . . ?" Gideon Hawke exclaimed.

The head of Lost Books had entered the gallery. He could see the devastation, and in another moment he would see the creature that had caused it.

"Something is loose in the museum!" cried Wolfus Bone.

"It's a flarewolf!" Hawke muttered.

The flarewolf bared its teeth.

Hawke reached inside his pocket and produced a Popper Stopper. "Just as well I brought this."

He pointed the glass phial at the slavering creature and removed the stopper. A milky-white vapor immediately surrounded the flarewolf. The creature threw back its head and flared again, scorching the air with its fiery breath. The force of its flames dispelled the white vapor, driving it back into the phial.

"It's too strong for an ordinary Popper Stopper," cried Wolfus Bone.

The creature let out a long, low howl. It fixed its eyes on the two men. It crouched low, ready to spring.

Wolfus Bone took a step back.

"Wait," cried Hawke. "The beast is strong, but it has not won yet."

He held the Popper Stopper to his mouth and whispered into it. The phial glowed yellow and regurgitated its white vapor, billowing out in a thick cloud like smoke. Once again the vapor surrounded the flarewolf, but this time it did not recede when the beast's flames touched it. The flarewolf's eyes glinted with malice. But in less than a second the vapor had been sucked back into its glass container, and the flarewolf with it.

"That's better," said Hawke.

Wolfus Bone looked relieved. "That was close," he said. "The dark magic that released the flarewolf is strong."

Gideon Hawke held up the glass phial in his hand. It was glowing red. "Yes," he mused. "The beast will have to be handled carefully. I will keep it in my study until it can be returned to its book."

On the other side of the door, Archie and Bramble heard the two men talking. Bramble removed her hat and looked at a large scorch hole. Archie put his finger to his lips and gestured to the other side of the door.

"That's made a mess," Gideon Hawke declared,

gazing around at the damage caused by the flarewolf. "But it could have been worse."

"Yes, it could," agreed Wolfus Bone. "It could have burned the museum down! But what released that foul creature? And why didn't it simply ezaporate, Gideon?"

"There is powerful dark magic at work here," said Hawke. He looked troubled. "And if we're right, then we can expect more of these attacks. We must arm ourselves. And I mean something more potent than Popper Stoppers. I have weapons in my study. Whatever released the flarewolf is very strong indeed."

Bone shook his head. "The disturbances began when Archie Greene began his apprenticeship. Almost to the day! I'm sure the boy is concealing a book and the dark magic is connected to it."

In the passageway out of sight, Archie's and Bramble's eyes met. Archie had a horrible feeling that Wolfus Bone was right. The trouble *had* started when he arrived. Had he brought the dark magic into the museum?

"It still doesn't mean that Archie is to blame for the attacks," Hawke objected.

"I'm not sure the boy knows the part he has played," said Bone. "Perhaps he is being used."

Archie had heard enough. More than enough. Was

he to blame for all the bad things that had happened since he arrived in Oxford? Maybe that was why Gran and his father had tried to keep him away from the museum. Was that what his father had discovered in the Book of Destiny?

CHAPTER 30

Magic Spills

The next day at work, Archie was still brooding over what he'd overheard. Was it possible that he had brought the dark magic into the museum without even knowing it?

When Old Zeb said he had a job for him to do, it was a welcome distraction.

"Take this repaired spell book back to Mortal Magic," the old man said. "And don't dawdle on the way."

Archie had noticed that the old bookbinder was finding lots of errands for him of late. Archie suspected that with Greaders at large, the old man thought it was better for him to spend more time with the other apprentices.

Ordinarily, Archie wouldn't have minded at all. He loved being at Mothballs. But after what he'd overheard Wolfus Bone say, he wondered whether it was such a good idea.

Archie collected the repaired spell book and was putting it in his bag when he noticed a scorch hole in the fabric. It must have have happened when the flarewolf was chasing them. His book was in the bag and he checked it for damage, but it appeared unharmed. He wondered about carrying the book around with him. But he didn't dare leave it anywhere.

When he arrived at the museum, the apprentices were going about their work. There had been no more attacks since the incident with the flarewolf, but there was a tense atmosphere, and everyone was being careful not to go anywhere alone.

The three department heads, Dr. Motley Brown, Feodora Graves, and Vincent von Herring, were a reassuring presence. The other Elders were also making themselves available to accompany apprentices if they needed to leave the main gallery. Outwardly, it was working. The museum seemed calm.

Yet no matter how hard he tried, Archie couldn't shift a nagging feeling that something bad was about to happen. He walked through the Great Gallery with a sense of dread. As he stared up at the side galleries, he half expected to see that the bookcases were empty or on fire.

Everyone was trying to put on a brave face. Rupert Trevallan was engrossed in research at one of the reading tables, studying a book about dark magical creatures. It was open on a page about vargs—unpleasant wolflike creatures. As Archie passed, Rupert made a claw shape with his hand and bared his teeth. Then he winked.

Archie grinned and kept walking. Above him, Bramble was balancing on a stepladder to reach one of the higher shelves. When she saw Archie, she held up a book about screaming banshees, waving precariously, and then pretended to lose her balance. Archie smiled at her antics.

Even Peter Quiggley, the new apprentice who had been attacked outside Quill's, was getting in on the act. A thin, fair-haired boy, he walked past with a wheelbarrow full of books about magical plants with a watering can perched on top.

"What?" he asked when he saw Archie's amused look. "They need repotting."

Archie allowed himself a small smile. He knew that they were all overcompensating, but outwardly at least, everyone seemed confident that the Museum Elders would come up with a plan to protect the magic books. Archie should have more faith in them. The museum had survived in Oxford for hundreds of years. It would last a few more years yet.

He was just thinking about all the changes that the museum must have seen when he heard a muffled cry behind him.

It was Peter Quiggley. His wheelbarrow was on its side, with the wheel still spinning. Archie thought it was another joke until he caught the frightened look on Peter's face. Then he realized what had scared him. Plants were sprouting from the magic books. A fast-growing ivy had twisted itself around Peter, its spiky-leafed branch winding itself around his waist, starting to squeeze him. As Archie watched, a blue rose extended its thorny arm and began to coil itself around Peter's shoulders, and an orange-trumpeted climber snaked its way toward the boy's feet.

"What's happening?" cried Archie, desperately trying to pry the climber off Peter.

"It's the books!" squeaked Peter. "They've gone wild!"

There was a crash from the galleries and another shout. Archie looked up to see that Rupert Trevallan's chair was overturned. Rupert was desperately backing away from the book on his table, which was making low growling sounds. Suddenly, a huge gray wolf leaped from the book, snarling and drooling. It began to stalk Rupert, its head low and its teeth bared.

"It's a varg!" Rupert yelled, picking up a chair and holding it in front of him. "Get help! Quick!"

But before Archie could react, there was a cry from above, followed by a high-pitched shrieking sound. The book that Bramble was holding snapped open, and out flew three ghostly hags with bloodless white faces and staring eyes. The banshees shimmered with a dull gray light, and their wailing was almost too terrible to bear. Bramble clung to the ladder with her arms and tried to cover her ears with her hands. The banshees soared into the air and shot off in all directions, tormenting the apprentices with their ghastly white faces and their high, wailing screams.

Books on the bookshelves were spontaneously disgorging their magical contents. A large volume leaped from the bookcase and exploded with flash of blue and stench of sulfur. A demon-faced gargoyle erupted from it and immediately sprang up onto the galleries and began pulling books from the shelves and throwing them into the air, adding to the chaos.

By now the Great Gallery was in a state of pandemonium, with apprentices running for their lives. The air was thick with all manner of vile creatures. They flapped and fluttered in the air like enormous moths. The empty covers of the books they had come from were all over the floor. Somewhere amid it all, someone was sobbing. Arabella Ripley crouched under a table with her hands clasped over her head.

"It's the grimoires!" she wailed. "They're releasing their spells!"

At that moment, an entire row of black books leaped from the shelf, flapped open their covers, and began ejecting vampire bats like some demonic firework display.

Bramble slid down the stepladder and was trying to fend off one of the banshees with a book. The book in her hands disappeared in a puff of black smoke, and when it cleared, she was holding a writhing snake. She screamed and dropped the snake, which slithered back toward her.

By now Rupert Trevallan was backed up against the wall, watching helplessly as a pack of vargs devoured a magic book, ripping it to shreds. Peter Quiggley had disappeared completely in a forest of writhing green ivy.

Archie felt his anger welling up inside him. He could hear dark voices calling from the magic books. He knew that he was the only one who could hear them and that he should do something. He had some sort of power with the whispering, but he didn't know what it was. If he tried to use his powers, he might make matters worse. But he had to try.

"Leave him alone," Archie cried, directing his voice at the vargs. The snarling animals stopped stalking Rupert for a moment and turned their fierce red eyes on him. The largest varg showed its teeth and gave a growl of warning.

"I said leave him alone," Archie tried again. But his voice sounded thin and unsure.

"There's nothing you can do, Archie," Rupert called out. "Go for help!"

On hearing his voice, the pack of vargs switched their attention back to Rupert.

Just then a banshee swooped past Archie's face, shrieking with laughter.

"Get away from me!" Archie cried. "Or I'll . . ." But he didn't know how to finish the threat.

"Or you'll what?" screeched the hag. "Whisper me to death! Ha! Ha! Ha!"

Archie felt a sudden surge of anger. "Yes," he cried through clenched teeth. "I would . . . if only I knew how!"

The hag soared into the air, cackling.

Archie gazed around in desperation. What was he supposed to do? Nothing he had tried had helped at all.

He was still desperately wondering what to do when the doors to the Great Gallery flew open. Gideon Hawke strode into the middle of the room, flanked by Wolfus Bone, who held a Popper Stopper in his hands. Bone pointed his phial at the rampaging gargoyle, releasing the white vapor. It curled around the creature, but it had no effect. The gargoyle leered maliciously and went on tossing books off the shelves.

Gideon Hawke's face looked like thunder. In his hands he held the hooked wooden staff that Archie had seen in his study.

"Return to your books," he cried, and he struck the ground three times with the staff. The mayhem continued unabated, but Hawke gave the command a second time.

"Return to your books or I will destroy you and the books you came from!"

The gargoyle leaped down from the gallery and swept a row of books onto the floor in defiance. Hawke pointed the staff at it. The gargoyle was engulfed in flames and turned to ash.

Hawke turned the staff on the banshees that were still screaming around the huge gallery. One by one, they were incinerated. The vampire bats received the same treatment.

There was a cry of fear from Rupert Trevallan as the vargs leaped at him, their teeth gnashing and their jaws snapping. Hawke wheeled around and pointed his staff again. The creatures were turned to ashes in midair.

"That was close," cried Rupert. "I thought I was varg meat there."

Hawke nodded, but his face was grim. There was a muffled squeak from behind him.

"Peter!" Archie cried. "He was attacked by the magic plants!"

They all turned to look at the tangle of branches and briars.

Hawke pointed the staff at the writhing green ivy. The snaking tendrils were turned to charcoal, leaving a smudge-faced Peter Quiggley gasping for air.

"You are safe for now," Hawke called out in a loud voice. "But all of you need to understand what we are dealing with. The dark magic is getting stronger. The creatures did not respond to the Book Hook's command. They preferred destruction to submitting to the staff. We cannot rely on it to stop them next time."

CHAPTER 31

Unanswered Questions

Archie was quiet on the way home. The latest attack on the museum had left him very shaken. This time the other apprentices had been in danger, not just him. Something was gnawing away at him, and he couldn't get it out of his head.

"Sounds like the attacks are getting worse," said Thistle when they told him what had been going on. "Whatever magic is causing it must be very powerful to control all those books at once. Where do you think it is coming from?"

"I still think Rusp's behind it," said Bramble. "I reckon he's using it to help him steal magic books."

"Well, I suspect the Ripleys," said Thistle. "They've been collecting magic books for generations. Perhaps Arabella is following in her grandfather's footsteps. What do you think, Arch?"

Archie didn't answer. He was too preoccupied with his own thoughts.

"What's up, Archie?" asked Bramble.

"Nothing," he said.

"I thought we said no more secrets?"

"I just feel guilty," Archie confessed. Since he and Bramble had overheard that whatever was attacking the museum might be linked to his book, they'd kept it locked up inside Archie's bag in case it caused any more trouble. But Archie still felt bad.

"What if Bone is right? What if I am responsible for the attacks on the museum? Perhaps it runs in the family." He couldn't stop himself blurting out his greatest fear. "What if my father was responsible for the fire at the museum twelve years ago?"

"No," said Thistle. "I checked with Dad. Alex Greene left the museum before the fire. Dad said there was a huge row over a missing book. Your dad was accused of taking it, and he had to leave."

"Oh, it gets better and better," said Archie. "So now

my dad's a book thief as well as an arsonist."

"But that's just it," said Thistle. "If he'd already left the museum, he couldn't have started the fire, could he?"

"Oh," said Archie. "I see what you mean. But it still doesn't explain why he stole a book. Why would he do that?"

"Hold on," said Bramble. "You're jumping to conclusions again, Arch. We don't know that he did take a book. And if he did, well . . ."

Archie raised his eyebrows. "You're going to say that he must have had a good reason, right?"

"Well, er, yes," said Bramble. "Just as you had a good reason for taking your book."

"But that doesn't make it right," said Archie. "It's still breaking the Lore. What if my book is what's causing the attacks on the museum?"

"We don't even know your book is evil," Bramble reassured him. "Perhaps it's one of the great books of magic."

"That's true," said Archie thoughtfully. He didn't say any more. But he made up his mind to find out once and for all.

The next day, Archie saw his chance. While the other apprentices and Elders were busy, he caught Bramble's eye.

"Psssst, Bram, I've got a plan. But I need you to watch my back."

"What are you going to do?" Bramble asked.

"I'm going to ask *The Book of Yore*."

"Archie, that really isn't a good idea," Bramble said. "You got away with it once, but apprentices aren't supposed to consult the magic books."

"That's because they're not book whisperers," Archie said. "Anyway, it's the only way to find out if the book is good or evil. Now, are you with me or not?"

"Of course I am. But I don't like it."

⌒

The two cousins slipped unseen into the Scriptorium. As before, the torches magically lit themselves when they entered. Archie approached *The Book of Yore*.

"Why didn't my father want me to know about magic?" he demanded.

He heard the rasping voice. "You have returned, book whisperer?"

"Yes," replied Archie. "I need answers."

"You have been warned before about the dangers of dwelling in the past," the voice rasped. "Your safety cannot be guaranteed."

"I understand," said Archie. "But I have to know why

my father tried to keep me away from the museum."

The Book of Yore flipped open and then slammed shut. A new bookmark had appeared among its pages.

"It is done. But there is still time to change your mind. Do you choose to consult the past?"

"Yes, I do," said Archie.

"So be it!"

Archie stepped forward and opened the book to the page with the bookmark.

The date was April 14, 1603—a month after his previous visit.

As Archie touched the page, the surface rippled as before, and he was drawn into the book. He heard Bramble gasp, and then he closed his eyes.

When he opened them again, he was back in the same book-lined room. He could see the old man sitting at the table as before. Archie now knew him to be John Dee. On the table in front of him was his book.

Sitting across the table from Dee was the same man as before. Again, Archie could not see his face.

"What have you discovered?" the man demanded of Dee.

Dee shook his head. "I want no more to do with you or this book," he declared angrily.

"But we had an agreement," said Dee's associate. "If I brought you the book, you would decipher its meaning."

"And I have done so," declared Dee, "but I will not share it with you or any other."

"We had a bargain!"

"And I have kept my part of that bargain," declared Dee angrily. "I gave you the book whisperer's name. In return you were supposed to bring me the book I desired."

"And so I did," said Dee's associate.

"This is no book of angels!" spat Dee. "It is a book of dark magic."

The other man laughed contemptuously. "Only a fool would expect anything else."

"Perhaps you are right," said Dee. "I was a fool to trust it, even though it is written in the language of the angels. But no one else will make the same mistake. I have sealed the book with a magical clasp of my own design. It will not permit the book to be opened by any other than a book whisperer."

The second man was silent while he contemplated this. When he finally spoke, it was with a sneer.

"It is just as well, then, that you have identified one for me."

"But that will not be for another four hundred years!" exclaimed Dee.

"Oh, but it will be worth the wait," taunted the man, snatching the book from the table. "The book will pass to the boy."

"No!" cried Dee, flying into a rage. "The book must be returned to the Museum of Magical Miscellany! It is the only place it will be safe."

"It is a little late for that," scoffed the other man. "Besides, I have a much better plan."

Dee's face turned pale. "What do you intend to do?"

"I have made inquiries at a London firm called Folly and Catchpole. They specialize in magical instructions, and they are very discreet. They will deliver the book to the boy at a future date."

Dee looked shocked. "But how will he know what it is?" he asked.

"Oh, he will find out," jeered the other man, "in due course."

"I forbid it!" roared Dee.

"You cannot prevent it!"

"Then I must warn the boy."

Dee made a lunge for the book, but the other man

was too quick. He leaped from his chair and ran from the room with it in his hands.

The room went dark, and Archie felt himself falling again.

———

When Archie opened his eyes, he was back in the Scriptorium.

"There you are!" cried Bramble. "I was starting to get really worried. What did you find out?"

"I think my book contains dark magic," said Archie.

"Even more reason to get out of here," cried Bramble. "Now come on."

"But I am so close to finding out what it is," said Archie. "I just need one more answer."

Bramble looked uncomfortable. "No, Archie. Even I know that you shouldn't mess with *The Book of Yore*. Let's find Gideon Hawke." She moved back toward the door. "Are you coming or not?"

Archie glanced up. "Er, yeah, I'm right behind you," he mumbled. Bramble opened the heavy wooden door and slipped out of the Scriptorium.

Archie was about to follow when *The Book of Yore* suddenly flew open again. Its pages ruffled. When it snapped shut, Archie saw a new bookmark had appeared.

"Your unspoken question is answered, book whisperer. But the danger increases each time you ask," said the raspy voice. Archie did not heed the warning—he was already opening the book. The date marked was July 26, 48 BC.

CHAPTER 32

The Book of Souls

When Archie opened his eyes, he was in a moonlit courtyard. The air was warm and smelled of the aromatic plants of the Mediterranean. In front of him was a magnificent stone building. Archie knew it was the Great Library of Alexandria.

A tall, dark figure was moving stealthily across the courtyard. Glancing furtively over his shoulder, he ducked into a concealed entrance. Archie was about to follow when he suddenly found himself inside the building. As he watched from behind a pillar, the same tall figure passed him. He was close enough now for Archie to see that he was a very tall man indeed, with a hooked nose and dull black eyes like a bird of prey. His dark eyes flashed in the shadows as if he could sense another presence, but he stared straight through Archie without seeing him.

The man lit a torch and hurried along a stone passageway. Archie followed him until they reached a heavy iron door. The man unlocked the door with a silver key. Archie just managed to slip through the door before the tall figure closed it behind him.

They were in a large, low-ceilinged room lined with books and scrolls. Seven books were chained to the wall at one end. The tall man opened the first of them. His lips moved as he read under his breath, and the room felt suddenly cold. Black shapes started to form in the shadows.

Suddenly, the door flew open and another man stood in the doorway. Dressed in a white robe, he was a tall man, too, but not as tall as the first. The two men locked eyes with each other.

"You dare to open the Terrible Tomes?" cried the man in white.

"Dare!" roared the other. "I wrote the greatest of them!"

"You know it is forbidden, Barzak! If you close the book now, then perhaps no great harm will come of it."

The dark-eyed man laughed aloud. "You are a bigger fool than I thought, Obadiah, if you think this is the first time I have opened the dark books!"

The man in white looked shocked. "It is you who are the fool," he cried, "if you think you can resist the Terrible Tomes."

"Why should I resist them?" cried Barzak. "In just a few more minutes they will be at my command!"

"I cannot allow that," said the man in white, his voice quiet now. "The beasts that guard the library have been woken. They will be here any moment. This is your last chance to give yourself up."

"Never," cried Barzak, and he hurled his flaming torch. A pile of tinder-dry scrolls exploded in flames, and the fire spread to one of the bookcases.

"You will destroy the library!" cried the man in white.

"The Terrible Tomes will not burn!" sneered Barzak. "You know that they are beyond flames."

"But the others . . . ?"

"Why should I care about the others?" roared Barzak. And as he did, a second bookcase erupted into flames.

By now the room was on fire, and Archie could barely see for the smoke. He couldn't breathe, and with a rising sense of panic, he realized that although no one could see him, he was trapped in the burning room.

The smoke stung his eyes, and the heat burned his lungs. Archie sank to his knees.

He had almost given up hope when he felt something hook his belt and give a sharp tug. The next thing he knew, he was back in the Scriptorium. Gideon Hawke was standing over him, holding one end of the Book Hook—the other end, with the hook, was still attached to Archie's belt.

"That was close," Hawke said. "Another few seconds and I wouldn't have been able to reach you. It's just a good thing that no one closed the book—and that your cousin had the sense to come and get me. Are you all right, you young fool?"

Archie was still spluttering and wheezing from the smoke, but he managed to nod.

"And now, Archie Greene, it is time for some straight talking. I have been very patient with you, but my patience is at an end." Hawke's eyes flashed with anger. "You have something for me? If you hand it over now, then I am prepared to take a lenient view. This, though, is your last chance, so I suggest you take it. The museum is already in great danger, and I cannot allow you to jeopardize it further. Enough of this foolishness—where is the book?"

"It's in my bag," Archie spluttered.

"Give it to me. Now!"

———

Half an hour later, Archie and Bramble were sitting in the Lost Books Department. Gideon Hawke was pacing up and down, his brow furrowed. Wolfus Bone was sitting in an armchair by the fire.

"This book you have been harboring is a very dangerous book indeed."

Archie looked sheepish. "I should have given it to you before. I thought I was protecting it. But now . . ."

Hawke's eyebrows twitched. "Yes?"

Archie raised his head. "Now I think it is responsible for the attacks on the museum!" he blurted out.

Hawke glowered at him. "Let's hope it's not too late to stop it. Now, go back to the beginning," he said, clearing himself a seat and sitting down. "I want you to tell me everything."

Archie told Hawke everything he could remember, from when Horace Catchpole had delivered the package until the moment Gideon Hawke had pulled him from *The Book of Yore*. The only information he held back was about him being a book whisperer. It seemed such an outrageous claim, and he didn't want to get into any more trouble than he was already in. When he had finished, he stared at his feet awkwardly. Hawke nodded.

"Good," he said. "Now that's out of the way, perhaps we can be friends."

"The book," Archie said. "What is it?"

"I believe it is Barzak's *Book of Souls*."

Bramble gasped.

"But how is that possible?" cried Archie. "I mean, it is written in Enochian script, the language of angels. Isn't that only used to write good magic?"

Hawke looked solemn. "Not quite," he said. "It is true that many of the great books of magic were written in the language of angels. But it was also used to write one of the Terrible Tomes. It was the script favored by the ancient magic writers. And that is exactly why Barzak chose it to write *The Book of Souls*. He wanted to disguise the book's true purpose."

"Well, it certainly fooled us!" exclaimed Bramble.

"But if you knew that I had it, why didn't you say anything?" asked Archie.

Hawke met his eye. "I could have forced you to surrender the book. But I believed that there was a reason it was sent to you. So I decided to wait and see what developed." He shook his head. "Besides, even I did not imagine for a second that it was Barzak's book!"

"Why is *The Book of Souls* so dangerous?" Archie asked.

Hawke did not reply at first. His brow was heavy, and he seemed lost in his own thoughts. The fire had died down. He picked up a log and placed it on the grate. The tinder-dry wood immediately caught, with bright-orange tongues of fire snaking out from the embers, licking its underside, curling and writhing in their hunger to consume the wood.

Hawke watched the flames for a moment.

"As you know, Alexander the Great entrusted his magical collection to the Flame Keepers. When Alexander died, they continued their work. Time passed.

"Three hundred years later, Barzak began to write dark magic, using Enochian script to hide what he was doing. When the chief librarian realized what Barzak was up to, he banished him. But by then it was too late—Barzak had already written *The Book of Souls,* a book of the darkest magic imaginable," said Hawke. "A magic so dark that it could bring down the heavens and destroy the earth!"

"We thought it was about talking to angels!" said Bramble lamely.

Hawke winced. "Others have made the same mistake, including John Dee. It is what Barzak intended. But the Terrible Tomes corrupt all who seek to use their power.

"Barzak thought he could control the dark magic he had created, but he had already fallen under its spell. The chief librarian locked away his book with the other Terrible Tomes. But Barzak couldn't keep away. He crept back into the Library of Alexandria and opened the room where the Tomes were kept. I am sure his intention was to release the magic and make himself its master. But the chief librarian discovered him. In the struggle, Barzak started a fire, and the Great Library of Alexandria was burned down."

"And Barzak? What happened to him?" Archie asked.

"He was consumed by the flames, but before he was, he swore he would have his revenge. He cursed the library, and he cursed the chief librarian and all his descendants."

Hawke paused. "The chief librarian's name was Obadiah Greene. Yes, Archie, your ancestor."

Archie's mouth fell open.

"What a strange coincidence," said Bramble, "that the

book should come to Archie when it was his ancestor who destroyed its author."

"If it was a coincidence," said Hawke darkly.

"But how does John Dee fit into any of this?" said Archie. "He came much later."

"That's right. John Dee was a collector as well as a magician," explained Hawke. "He spent half his life trying to track down the lost books from Alexandria. This book was his greatest discovery. Or so he thought.

"But Dee mistook the purpose of *The Book of Souls*. He thought it would allow him to speak to angels."

"We think it was Dee who sent me the riddle," Archie said. "It had his symbol on it—do you think it's important?"

"We shouldn't discount it," said Gideon. "I'll have the Elders look into it."

At that moment, there was a commotion in the hall outside Hawke's study, and Vincent von Herring strode into the room.

"Gideon, Wolfus. What's all this I hear about one of the Terrible Tomes being found?"

"We believe we have recovered *The Book of Souls*," said Gideon Hawke.

"Barzak's book?" cried von Herring. "Good heavens! How long have you known about this?"

Archie glanced nervously at Hawke. He wondered if he was about to get into a lot of trouble.

"We've had our eye on it for some time," answered Hawke, "thanks to Archie here."

"Good work, Gideon," said von Herring. "I don't normally approve of apprentices getting involved with dangerous books, but well done, Archie." His eye alighted on the book on Hawke's desk. "Is that it?" he said.

Hawke nodded. "Yes. But it will have to go through the proper procedures to be certain that it is what we believe it is. I have sent for Morag."

"There's no time for that, Gideon!" exclaimed von Herring. "If it is *The Book of Souls*, then we cannot afford to take any chances. I will put it in the Crypt immediately."

"But we should wait until Morag has researched the book in the Archive," cried Wolfus Bone.

Von Herring looked at him. "Whatever is the matter, Wolfus?"

"I need more time to study it. To be absolutely certain."

Von Herring gave him a sharp look. "Do you think that's wise, Wolfus? Surely you and Gideon know better than anyone that the Terrible Tomes have a corrupting influence?"

"But there are procedures that must be followed, particularly with a book of this power," Bone protested. "I need more time."

"We don't have more time," said von Herring. "The museum is under attack. We can't leave it to chance. If it is one of the seven, then it must be locked in the Crypt. As the head of Dangerous Books, I absolutely insist on it. I will take it there myself. Immediately."

Before anyone could stop him, von Herring had picked up the book and marched out of Gideon Hawke's study.

CHAPTER 33

The Hourglass

Word had spread among the apprentices that one of the Terrible Tomes had been recovered. Their relief was tempered by the knowledge that the museum was still on maximum alert, because the Elders feared that an attack by Greaders was imminent. Some apprentices had not come back to work, although most had decided to return. Archie and Bramble were among them.

Old Zeb remained wary. "Now that *The Book of Souls* is locked away in the Crypt, let's hope that's the last of it," the old bookbinder said. "But I can't believe that you kept it a secret from me for so long, Archie."

"Sorry," said Archie, feeling embarrassed. "I didn't

realize how dangerous it was. But at least it explains what the Greaders were after."

"Hmm," muttered the old man. "I suppose so, but Gideon Hawke says the danger is not passed yet. He believes the Greaders are still plotting to attack the museum."

"Attack—how?" asked Archie.

"I don't know," said Old Zeb. "But Gideon says we must remain on our guard. He suggested that the apprentices brush up on their knowledge of dark magic just in case. Now, take these Popper Stoppers to the museum. We don't want any magic going astray with Greaders at large."

"Did he mention the riddle?"

"No," said Old Zeb. "But you can leave it to the Elders now. We are meeting later today to discuss plans to defend the museum."

Archie was still thinking about the riddle when he arrived at the museum.

Most of the apprentices were in the Great Gallery. Archie spotted Rupert Trevallan and asked him what to do with the glass phials.

"A mammoth, you say?" said Rupert. "I'll take that one to the menagerie. But Sir Bodwin will have to go to central phialing. Ask Enid about that. She's in charge of magical remnants now."

Archie thanked him. He'd give the other phial to Enid when he saw her. Gideon Hawke had mentioned dark magic to Old Zeb. He must think that another attack was likely. Archie sat at a desk and opened *A Survivor's Guide to Black-Hearted Beasts & Beings*. He looked up flarewolf.

FLAREWOLF: Distantly related to werewolves, flarewolves are part wolf and part dragon. In common with other dark beasts, a flarewolf can be destroyed only with a magical weapon (for more on magical weapons, see the *Compendium of Magical Instruments*).

Archie scanned the bookshelves until he found the *Compendium of Magical Instruments*. What was the name of the black dagger he had seen in Gideon Hawke's study? Hawke had called it a Shadow Blade. He thumbed through the book until he found the entry.

SHADOW BLADE: A Shadow Blade is a magical weapon that has captured the reflection of pure light in the night sky—usually a moonbeam or starlight—and retains its power. Because they can penetrate any darkness, Shadow Blades are useful to destroy dark spirits (for more on dark spirits, see *A Survivor's Guide to Black-Hearted Beasts & Beings, Vol. I*). Most Shadow Blades are made from obsidian, the black glass forged in the heat of a volcano, or other materials that do not reflect light, such as ebony and jet.

He was about to close the book when he realized that a page had been neatly folded over at the corner.

IMAGINING GLASS: Sometimes mistaken for an ordinary magnifying glass, an Imagining Glass is a magical instrument that magnifies the imagination of the person who looks through it. The words "imagination" and "magic" are closely linked, and many leading authorities (including Gideon Hawke from the Museum of Magical Miscellany in Oxford) argue that human imagination represents the last vestige of the magical power we all once possessed.

Archie read the entry again. He had never realized that reference books could be so interesting.

He was rereading the description of the blade when

he heard a hissing sound, like air leaking. He shrugged and continued with his task. But the sound persisted.

It was coming from the Scriptorium. Archie eased the door open and the torches instantly flared to life, dispelling the darkness. The hissing sound was coming from the glass dome, but now it sounded more like water running.

Archie crossed the room and climbed the wooden steps up onto the viewing platform. As he peered through the glass, the color drained from his face. He raced off to get help.

Gideon Hawke, Wolfus Bone, and Morag Pandrama came immediately. The other department heads joined them.

"*The Book of Reckoning*!" shrieked Morag Pandrama. Sand was pouring through the crystal hourglass.

"But that's impossible!" Wolfus Bone gasped.

Gideon Hawke stared at the book. "No," he whispered. "Not impossible, but very unfortunate. It is as I feared—the books are preparing to release their magic."

"How long do you think we have, Gideon?" Bone asked.

Hawke stared at the hourglass. "A few hours at most."

When he met Thistle in front of Quill's a few minutes later, Archie told him about *The Book of Reckoning*. Thistle's face turned pale.

"That's not good!" Thistle exclaimed.

"No," agreed Archie. "The Museum Elders are meeting right now to decide what to do."

"That explains why I saw all the apprentices coming out early," said Thistle. "Where's Bram?"

"She's just behind me. She stopped to talk to Rupert."

"The Elders will think of something," said Thistle, trying to sound confident.

"Maybe," mused Archie. "But I can't help thinking John Dee's riddle is important in all this. I'm sure it must mean something."

Just then Bramble caught up with them. "I know what's behind the blue door!" she announced breathlessly. "And you won't believe it when you hear! I asked Rupert if he'd ever heard of a creature with amber eyes. He said he'd do some digging around for me, and he just gave me this." She showed them a note. "It's taken from an entry in *Encyclopaedia Animalia Rarium*.

"The creature Archie saw is a Bookend Beast! And there are two of them. They are made of stone and guard treasure and other precious objects. They are found on ancient tombs and that sort of thing."

"But the creature I saw wasn't made of stone, it was very much alive," said Archie.

"Yes, the Bookend Beasts can come to life if what they are guarding is threatened. And when they do, their eyes glow amber. And another thing: the last-known pair of Bookend Beasts protected the magic books at the Great Library in Alexandria—and they were in the form of griffins."

"Which means each has the body of a lion and the head and wings of an eagle!" Archie said. "Bram, are you thinking what I'm thinking? About the riddle?"

"Now the two of you are talking in riddles!" complained Thistle. "What are you talking about?"

"The riddle," breathed Bramble excitedly.

> *"Buried deep in caverns cold*
> *A secret that remains untold*
> *Two ancient sentries guard the prize*
> *With lion heart and eagle eyes."*

"Now I get it," Thistle exclaimed. "It's referring to the Bookend Beasts!"

Bramble smiled. "Yes, and there's something else

about them. They can talk! Several people have reported holding conversations with them. They must be guarding something enormously powerful. That's what they do. But what?"

Archie grabbed his bag. "Like you always say, Bram, there's only one way to find out!"

"Hold on a minute," said Thistle. "I thought we agreed to let Gideon Hawke handle it from here? It could be really dangerous."

"Hawke's in the meeting of the Museum Elders," Archie said. "Von Herring says they aren't to be disturbed under any circumstances. So it's up to us!"

CHAPTER 34

Reading in the Dark

A rchie opened the door to the Aisle of White slowly so
that the bell wouldn't clang. There was no sign of
Marjorie as the three cousins crept along the aisles of
books and through the velvet curtain.

When they reached the bookcase where Archie had
heard the books whispering before, he paused.

"Hello, there," he said urgently. "You've got to talk to
me. I need your help!"

"I am very weak," *The Little Book of Blessings* said.
"We all are."

"I'm sorry I didn't do more to protect you when you
asked for my help, but I didn't understand the danger. It

was my book that was stealing your magic, wasn't it?"

"Yes," whispered *The Little Book of Blessings*. "I tried to warn you."

Archie nodded sadly. "I thought my book was in danger. Now I realize it *was* the danger!"

"Yes," said the little book. "Why have you come now?"

"I am a book whisperer," Archie said. "It is my duty to protect the magic books."

"You are going to face the Beasts, aren't you?"

Archie looked away. "Yes," he breathed. "Do you know what secret they guard?"

"They guard another entrance to the Crypt, and there is another secret, but I don't know what it is," said the little book. "But take me with you, and I will bring you luck."

Archie had a feeling he would need all the luck he could get. He slipped the little book into his back pocket.

"Bless you, Archie Greene. May you have the courage when the time comes."

The three cousins hurried down the stone stairs. When they reached the blue door, Archie reached down a torch from its bracket, then took a deep breath and turned the invisible door handle.

The Bookend Beast stood motionless. It was eight feet tall and carved from a single slab of gray stone. It had the head of a giant eagle, with a fearsome hooked beak and staring eyes. Below its neck, it had the muscular body of a lion, with chiseled fur that grew thick about its chest and flanks. Two huge feathered wings were folded across its back.

"Stay here," Archie said to Bramble and Thistle. "It's best if only one of us tries to talk to it."

As he stepped closer, the creature's eyes lit up a deep amber color.

"Uh-oh," whispered Thistle. "I think you woke it up."

With a sound like stone grinding on stone, the beast turned its head and held Archie with its gaze. A ripple of light pulsed through the beast, and its body turned from gray stone to living flesh. Archie felt his legs turn to jelly. He took a deep breath.

"Greetings, mighty Bookend Beast," he cried as loudly as he dared. His thin voice bounced off the walls and disappeared into the gloom.

The griffin flexed its enormous talons. When it spoke, its voice was deep and resonated in the darkness.

"Who are you who trouble me in my lair?" it thundered.

"I am Archie Greene," Archie replied. "Apprentice at

the Museum of Magical Miscellany. And this is Bramble Foxe and her brother, Thistle."

"And what is your reason for disturbing me, Archie Greene?"

"I have come on a matter of great urgency," Archie cried, projecting his voice into the void.

"You humans are always in such a hurry," the creature sighed, and Archie detected a great sadness in its voice. "Look at all the harm your urgency has done in the world." It shook its great eagle head slowly from side to side.

Archie felt his courage start to waver, but he stood his ground. "Mighty Bookend Beast, protector of secrets, I understand that you have a low opinion of humans," he empathized.

"Some humans," the creature boomed, "not all. But most are not worth the effort. I fear that any wisdom or magic your kind ever had has long since been forgotten."

"But that's what I must talk to you about," said Archie, seeing an opportunity to turn the conversation in his direction. "I need your help to protect the magic books that remain."

"You humans and your magic books. For centuries

my kind have guarded your treasures for you."

"What is it that you guard here?" Bramble asked, plucking up her courage.

The griffin lifted its head and shook its mighty wings. "This audience is at an end! You may leave now and live. But if you remain, then I will pass judgment on you."

Archie sensed that something had made the creature angry and that they were in grave danger.

"We would leave if we could," he cried. "But something terrible will happen if we can't prevent it!"

Archie knew this was his last chance. He took a deep breath.

"There is a great secret that only you can unlock," he cried. He thought that the creature's curiosity was his best hope. "But if you have grown old and forgetful, then I will leave you to your slumber."

He started to edge his way back toward his cousins.

"Wait." The creature's voice echoed in the stone cavern. "What is this secret of which you speak?"

"It is a riddle that only you know the answer to."

"Tell me this riddle," the beast commanded.

Archie recited the words that he had memorized. They echoed as he spoke them.

"Buried deep in caverns cold
A secret that remains untold
Two ancient sentries guard the prize
With lion heart and eagle eyes."

The griffin was silent. Archie tried again.

"Two ancient sentries guard this prize
With lion heart and eagle eyes.

"That is you!" cried Archie.

The creature bowed its great eagle head solemnly. "Indeed," it boomed. "It is a description of my brother and me. Who wrote this riddle?"

"It was written a very long time ago," Archie said. "By a man who wanted to keep his secrets safe. He hid them in a special place. His name was John Dee. Do you remember him?"

The beast bowed its head again. "Yes, I remember him. We promised the magician that none would pass without the secret word. Do you know the secret word?"

Archie thought hard. He recited the second half of the riddle.

"In stony silence shadows sleep
The final gift is safe to keep
To pass requires a simple test
Name the one whom I served best.

"'Name the one whom I served best?' I know this. Who did Dee serve? Dee served Queen Elizabeth," Archie said.

"Is that your answer?"

"No," said Archie. "Dee wouldn't have called her that."

The Enochian script danced before his eyes. Something was lodged in the deep recesses of his memory. If only he could remember what it was.

"Archie, try this," said Bramble. She pulled the Imagining Glass from her pocket. Archie peered at the Bookend Beast through the pink lens. He closed his eyes in concentration. When he opened them again, something glinted in his mind.

"Dee had a nickname for Queen Elizabeth. I read it in a book. Gloriana. That's what Dee called her. Gloriana is the answer."

"That is correct!" the Bookend Beast thundered. "That is the password."

Archie breathed a sigh of relief.

"But there is another test!"

Archie looked up to see a second Bookend Beast looming toward him out of the shadows. When the two beasts stood next to each other, it was clear that they were a set—like bookends for keeping books upright on a shelf. Except that they were eight feet tall.

"Another test!" cried Archie.

"Yes," said the second beast. "The magician said that only the book whisperer was allowed to pass. Are you he?"

"Yes, I am," said Archie.

"Prove it!" thundered the beast.

Archie looked at his cousins desperately. "How can I prove it?"

"I don't know," said Thistle. "Talk to a magic book or something."

Archie felt his hope ebbing away. Then suddenly he heard a voice. It sounded soft like tissue paper.

"Archie Greene is a book whisperer. And although he does not quite believe in himself yet, he could be a great book whisperer—perhaps the greatest ever!"

He had forgotten about *The Little Book of Blessings*!

"Thank you," he mumbled.

Bramble and Thistle looked at him blankly.

"They cannot hear me," said *The Little Book of Blessings*.

"But we can," thundered the first Bookend Beast. "You have passed the second test. But only you may pass beyond this point."

"But what about my cousins?" said Archie. "They are Flame Keepers, too."

The creatures shook their heads. "Only the book whisperer may pass."

They stood barring the way.

"We're not leaving you down here with those things," said Bramble.

"There's no other way," said Archie. "Wait for me in the bookshop. I have to do this."

The Bookend Beasts stood aside, and Archie stepped into the shadows.

CHAPTER 35

Last Writes

Dusk was falling when Bramble and Thistle slipped back through the velvet curtain and into the Aisle of White. An owl hooted nearby.

"This place is seriously creepy at night," whispered Thistle, peering out of the door into the courtyard toward Quill's.

"Don't be such a wimp!" snorted Bramble. She glanced at the bookcases. Thistle was right. It was creepy in the bookshop at night.

"Bram," whispered Thistle. He felt the hairs on the back of his neck rising. "I've got a horrible feeling something is watching us."

There was a movement outside in the courtyard. "What was that?" asked Bramble.

"There's someone out there!" exclaimed Thistle. A dark figure was moving stealthily toward the shop.

"Quick," Bramble said, "lock the door!"

"I can't," said Thistle. "Archie took the key. What are we going to do?"

"Hide!" whispered Bramble. She darted off to the right, her head down, staying in the shadows.

Thistle plunged left into the darkness. Hiding in the gloom, he watched the door.

The door slowly opened, and the floorboards creaked as someone crept up the aisle. A figure lunged at him in the darkness. Thistle dived to his right, eluding its grasp. His assailant tripped in the darkness and went sprawling on the floor.

Thistle could still hear it cursing as it scrambled back to its feet. A voice called out.

"Stop! I won't hurt you!"

Thistle saw Bramble's face appear out of the dark. "Run, Thistle, run!" she cried over her shoulder as she raced away up another aisle.

Thistle ran blindly, zigzagging between the book-cases. He glanced over his shoulder, and as he did his foot caught on a rug. He landed on his back with a bone-crunching thump. Everything went black.

~

Archie walked on in the shadows. Behind him now, the torch that lit the lair of the Bookend Beasts was just a faint glow. In front of him was a low entrance. It was far too small for the huge beasts to follow, but just big enough for him to squeeze through. Archie dropped to his hands and knees and crawled forward into the darkness. Water dripped down the walls. Archie's hands touched flagstones, and he stood up. Ahead, he could see another torch burning in the gloom and a green glow.

Archie heard a low, wheezing cough, like wind through dry bones. Someone was already there, waiting in the shadows.

~

When Thistle awoke, it was pitch-dark. He tried to sit up. His head was thumping. He touched the back of his skull and felt a large egg-shaped bump. Then he heard a voice. "You should have given us the book when you first had the chance."

He looked up to see Wolfus Bone bent over him with a black dagger in his hand.

Thistle screamed.

Bone put his finger to his lips. "There's no need be afraid," he said. "I have come to protect you. Gideon told me to find the three of you and keep you safe."

Bramble's face appeared over Bone's shoulder, pale but unharmed.

"It's all right, Thistle," she said. "Wolfus is here to help."

"Gideon had to attend the emergency meeting with the other Museum Elders, so he sent me," Bone continued. "He told me to bring you to the museum."

CHAPTER 36

The Ghost Writer

Archie stepped forward into the torchlight. The first thing he saw was the green glow. Then he saw the ghost of the old man. He knew he must be a ghost because of the way he shimmered in the light and was no more substantial than mist. His shoulders were stooped with age. His hair was pure white, and he had a thick white beard that reached down to his chest. He wore a long coat with a white fur collar. Archie recognized him.

"You are John Dee, aren't you?" he said.

A pained expression passed across the old man's face, as if he was trying to remember something from long ago.

"Dee?" he said. "Yes, that is my name. I have not heard

it spoken in so long that I had almost forgotten. Four hundred years I have haunted this place. It is my punishment." He sighed sadly. "For this is of my own making. I was foolish to believe that I might converse with the angels. It was my vanity that led me to this pass. What is your name, boy?"

"Archie Greene."

The ghost of John Dee peered at him in the gloom. "Then you are the one!" it cried. "It was to you that the book has passed. You are the one I saw in the scrying crystal."

———

Wolfus Bone strode down the corridor with his eyes fixed straight ahead. Gideon Hawke had told him to protect Archie and his cousins, and that was what he was going to do. But where was Archie? These were the thoughts running through his mind as he marched Bramble and Thistle toward the Lost Books section. He'd already lost precious time persuading Pink to let Thistle through the Permission Wall without a firemark.

He opened the door to Gideon Hawke's study. Something didn't feel right. His eyes were drawn to the desk where he had left the Popper Stopper containing the flarewolf. The glass phial was smashed on the floor. The magic clasp that he had used to lock it had been cast aside. Bone shook his head angrily.

Who would do such a thing?

His thoughts were interrupted by a blood-chilling howl. It was followed by a woman's screams coming from the Archive. The Archive was next to the Crypt.

"It's another attack," cried Bone, turning to the children. "Someone has released the flarewolf. You stay here."

"No way," said Bramble. "It's our museum, too, and we're coming with you!"

"I cannot guarantee your safety."

"We know that," said Thistle, "but we're coming anyway!"

Bone knew there was no point in arguing. "Very well," he said. "But stay with me."

He broke into a run. Bramble and Thistle ran after him, trying to keep up. The black blade glinted in his hand in the torchlight.

Bone threw open the door to the Archive. The room was a mess. The bookcases had been knocked over, and there were scrolls and papers smoldering all over the floor. Morag Pandrama was crouched in a corner, her hair scorched and her arms raised as if to ward off some unseen attacker.

"That thing!" she wailed. "It was here!"

"The flarewolf! Where is it now, Morag?"

"It is trying to get into the Crypt, Wolfus. We have to stop it! You have to get help!"

Bone sniffed the air. It was no more than a whiff of sulfur, but he sensed the creature lurking at the end of the passageway.

"It's too late for that," he said quietly.

Vincent von Herring suddenly appeared beside them. "What's all the screaming about?" he demanded. "How are the Museum Elders supposed to hold a meeting with all that racket going on?"

"It's the flarewolf," said Bone. "Someone released it, and now it's trying to get into the Crypt."

Von Herring looked alarmed. "We must raise a search party and destroy it once and for all."

"There's no time for that," said Bone. "Look!"

Two yellow eyes were watching them from the end of the corridor. The flarewolf threw back its head and howled. Then it leaped at them. As it did, Wolfus Bone threw himself in its path and caught it a glancing blow with the Shadow Blade. The beast howled in rage, shooting flames from its nostrils. For a moment it regarded them coldly; then it seemed to suddenly lose interest and bounded off down the corridor.

"You've scared it off," cried von Herring.

"No," said Bone. "We aren't its prey. It's going after Archie. Keep the other two children safe."

Von Herring placed a protective hand on Bramble's and Thistle's shoulders. "Very well, Wolfus," he said. "I will look after them."

"I will protect Archie," Bone said. "He is in great danger." Then he turned and ran after the flarewolf.

CHAPTER 37

The Keep Safe

In the gloom of the underground cavern, Archie stared at the ghost of John Dee.

"Why are you here?"

"I made a terrible mistake," said the ghost.

"Yes, I know," said Archie. "Gideon Hawke told me."

Dee hung his head. "I am so very sorry. I should never have involved you in all this. I cannot rest until *The Book of Souls* is safely returned to the museum and this great wrong is righted. But let me look at you. You must be the book whisperer I saw. Here," he said, indicating the silver pendant on its chain. In the center was a green gemstone, which was giving off the dull green aura. "It is my scrying crystal. It is very powerful. It allows its owner to see the past, the present, and the future. It is yours now. Take it."

Archie felt the weight of the pendant in his open hand.

"It comes with a warning, though," Dee's ghost said. "No man should see too far into the future. It is a lesson I have learned the hard way. Use the crystal only when it is absolutely necessary. And never, ever use it to see your own destiny."

"It's brought you nothing but misery," Archie said, gazing at the green gemstone in his hand. "I don't think I want it."

"Very wise," said the ghost. "Your wisdom tells me that you are exactly the right person to have it. But understand, Archie, there are others who will not respect the pendant's power as you do. They must not get their hands on it. That's why I have kept it hidden all these years. I give it to you as your Keep Safe. It will protect you."

Still Archie hesitated. "Take it," urged Dee. "You will need it."

Reluctantly, Archie took the pendant and hung it around his neck.

Dee's ghost nodded approvingly. "There are two other things that I must tell you. The first is that no Greader can resist the temptation to possess the pendant. Its power is too great. But anyone who tries to take it by force and breaks the chain is cursed by it.

"The second thing you need to know is that you are more powerful than you realize. The magic clasp on the book will obey a direct command from you." He paused. *"The Book of Souls*—where is it now?"

"It is locked in the Crypt with the other Terrible Tomes," Archie said.

A look of horror passed across Dee's face. "No!" he cried. "That's what it craves. It wants to be with the others! But it must be kept away from them!"

Archie's heart sank. "Then I have to stop it," he said.

"No," cried Dee, alarmed. "Not you, Archie. You of all people must not go in there."

But Archie was already running on into the shadows.

⌒

Wolfus Bone pursued the flarewolf through the dark corridors of the museum, his eyes fixed on the beast as it loped along in front of him.

As he entered one of the smaller galleries, he was met with a wall of flame, scorching the side of his face and his side. The flarewolf sprang at him, sending him sprawling and knocking the blade from his hand. Bone lay on his back like some giant insect unable to right itself.

He could do nothing as the creature's salivating jaws closed on his throat. With his last breath Bone reached out for the Shadow Blade. His long fingers grasped for it in the darkness and felt its cold touch. Drawing it into the palm of his hand, in one upward motion he plunged the blade through the flarewolf. It felt like his hand was passing through fire. The flarewolf gave a high-pitched howl. It twisted and turned on the blade. Darkness spilled from it, like fetid subterranean fog. Neither liquid nor vapor, it oozed from the creature and evaporated in the light.

Wolfus Bone lay on his back, gasping for air. He felt his own life draining away from him. His side where the creature had wounded him ached with a dull pain. His head throbbed and his sight was blurred. He heard a sound, and someone knelt down beside him. He was too weak to see who it was, but he felt them wipe the darkness from his eyes.

"Where is the flarewolf?" Bone asked.

"You have destroyed it," the voice said soothingly.

A cup was held up to his mouth, and he heard a voice whisper, "Drink this. It will ease your pain."

Bone opened his eyes and looked up into the face of Arabella Ripley. She smiled.

CHAPTER 38

The Crypt

Archie held the pendant aloft so that its green glow lit his way. Before him were seven marble plinths, a large iron cage on each. Four of the cages contained books whose covers were shut tight. But the fifth plinth was empty, and the door of its cage was open.

A man stood beside it. In one hand he held a set of silver keys, and in the other he clutched *The Book of Souls*. An eerie blue light spilled from it.

"Professor von Herring," Archie cried. "Thank goodness you're here. But aren't you supposed to be at the meeting with the Museum Elders?"

Von Herring smiled. "I left the meeting to look for

you. Now that I have found you, everything is going to be all right."

"But Professor," Archie said, "you don't understand— *The Book of Souls* wants to be with the other Terrible Tomes. That's what it wanted all along. It's trying to release their magic. We have to stop it."

Von Herring gave him a pitying look. "No, Archie, it's you who don't understand. *The Book of Souls* is where it was always supposed to be—and now that you are here, too, we can begin."

"Wha-what? But we have to protect the museum," Archie said, backing away.

"How very touching," said a voice behind him. Archie spun around and saw a figure standing in the shadows. Something was very wrong.

"Who are you?" Archie demanded.

"Come now, boy, surely you recognize the greatest magical book collector the world has ever known," the man sneered. Archie felt his stomach give a sickening twist as he recognized the cold gray eyes.

"You're Arabella's grandfather! But it can't be," he gasped. "Arthur Ripley is dead!"

The man laughed. "That's what I wanted you to believe. When I escaped from the fire, I was barely alive.

It took me years to recover, but now I'm ready to claim my greatest prize—*The Book of Souls*."

"But how do you know about the book . . . ?"

"It's really very simple," said Ripley. "John Dee's associate was my ancestor Morton Ripley, and he left a record of all their dealings. While I was recovering from my injuries, I found it among the papers at Ripley Hall. Morton had arranged for *The Book of Souls* to be delivered to you on your twelfth birthday. He knew that one of the Ripley family would be there to collect the book and collect you—because you see, Archie, you were always part of the plan. You still don't understand, do you?" Ripley laughed. "I came back for *The Book of Souls*. But the book on its own is no use to me. My ancestor realized that when he found it in the collection at Ripley Hall.

"He knew that only a gifted book whisperer could reveal its secrets, and there hadn't been one of those for centuries. So when he heard that the great magician John Dee was searching for the book, he had a brilliant idea. Dee was famous for his scrying skills. Why not use him to find the next great book whisperer?

"The second part of his plan was even more brilliant. He instructed Folly and Catchpole to deliver the book to you so that you and *The Book of Souls* would arrive together.

"On the day the book was supposed to be delivered, we were waiting—my accomplice and I. But you didn't show up, and that idiot Screech didn't know where the book was, so I had to be patient. Of course, we couldn't allow Screech to go around blabbing about what we were up to, so we kept him quiet."

"But why did you grab Peter Quiggley?" demanded Archie. "He knew nothing about it."

"Yes, well, one apprentice looks much like another," said Ripley. "We thought he was you, but it soon became clear that he was clueless, so we threw the little shrimp back. And now you are here."

Archie stepped away. He felt sick to his stomach. He realized he was caught in a trap.

Arthur Ripley smiled. "And now you are here and you *will* command it to release its last and greatest secret."

"Never!" cried Archie defiantly.

"You will do as you are told," von Herring ordered.

"And if I refuse?"

Ripley gave a cruel laugh. "Oh, you won't refuse," he said. "Because if you do, your cousins will die."

As he spoke, Von Herring pushed Bramble and Thistle forward. Their hands were bound and they were gagged. Archie stared into their wide, frightened eyes.

"So you see, Archie, you really have no choice," said von Herring. He handed the silver keys to Ripley and carefully placed *The Book of Souls* on the ground.

"You will command the book if you value your cousins' lives."

Archie stared desperately at Bramble's and Thistle's faces.

"All right," Archie said. "But what makes you think I can even open the book?"

"Because you are a book whisperer," said von Herring. "You opened it before. Now, hurry. It won't take the Museum Elders long to realize that I am not at the meeting, and they will come looking for us."

Archie gazed at *The Book of Souls*. Its cover was secured by the silver clasp with John Dee's symbol etched on it. He knew what the symbol meant now. It was a warning. The old magician had not wanted the book to be opened, but Archie had no choice.

"Open!" he commanded under his breath. "My cousins are depending on me."

With a click, the clasp opened. The strap with the clasp slithered onto the ground, and the book's cover sprang open.

"Command the book to release its last secret!" demanded Ripley. "Do it!"

Archie felt his panic rising. "But I don't know how," he said.

"I am disappointed in you, Archie. But since you have chosen to be so stubborn, I have no choice." He turned to von Herring. "Feed them to *The Book of Souls*!"

Archie saw the frightened look on Bramble's face as von Herring pushed her roughly toward the open book. As he did, *The Book of Souls* grew until it was several times its original size. Its surface shimmered like a pool of dark water. Bramble tried to struggle, but von Herring was too strong.

"Wait," cried Archie. "Don't hurt her. Tell me what I have to do. . . ."

Von Herring did not answer. His eyes were fixed on the pendant around Archie's neck. "That pendant," he said. "It is John Dee's scrying crystal. I recognize it from the portraits. Where did you get it? Give it to me."

He snatched the pendant from around Archie's neck, breaking the silver chain. The green crystal pulsed once, and Archie felt a sudden foreboding.

The Book of Souls was glowing with a strange blue light. The open pages rippled like the surface of a black lake. "Get back," he cried to his cousins. "Stand away from the book."

Bramble and Thistle pulled back, but von Herring

was rooted to the spot, staring into the crystal. His eyes were wide. His face suddenly changed. Confusion replaced delight. "But what is this? What is happening? No, not me. Take the girl," he screamed. The pendant fell from his hand, clattering onto the flagstone floor, and Archie picked it up.

The surface of the book began to churn. Two clawlike hands reached out and seized von Herring. He didn't even have time to scream before he disappeared beneath the surface of the pages.

Arthur Ripley shook his head. "He was a fool," he sneered. "He should have known that *The Book of Souls* would require something in exchange for releasing its secret. And now it has his soul. And if you refuse to cooperate, then your cousins are next!"

Ripley pushed Thistle forward. "So what do you say now, Archie Greene? Are you ready to do as you are told?"

Archie had no choice if he was to save his cousin.

"Whatever secret you still contain, I command you to reveal it."

There was a hissing sound, and black letters began to appear above *The Book of Souls*. The letters twisted into words.

Archie knew that it was dark magic, but he was unable to stop himself uttering the words.

"Let darkness fall
  Let darkness reign
  The power that was
  Shall rise again."

The Book of Souls began to shake violently. Its cover, which was stretched tight, started to ripple and bulge as if something were trapped inside. Shapes appeared in its surface. Suddenly, a dark, inky liquid erupted from the book like a volcano.

At first, it oozed like molten black clay, but gradually it began to take the form of a tall and very angular man in a long purple robe. Around his neck he wore a ruby gemstone on a silver chain. His face was deeply lined, and he had hollow cheeks and a long hooked nose. His white skin was the gnarled texture of the book's cover.

Long black hair threaded with silver framed his gaunt face, and his staring black eyes seethed with malice.

Archie had seen that face before.

"It can't be!" he exclaimed in horror.

"Oh yes it can," Ripley cried, his voice exultant. "The book's last secret is the soul of Barzak himself!"

CHAPTER 39

The Last Secret

Barzak was almost seven feet tall and towered over the others as he took in his surroundings. The Dark Warlock clenched his clawlike hands. His black fingernails curled at the ends, like talons.

Ripley's voice was triumphant. "You see, Archie, when he was caught in the fire, Barzak did the only thing he could to survive—he gave his soul to *The Book of Souls*. But he needed a book whisperer to release him—and now he is free!"

The warlock snapped his fingers, and *The Book of Souls* pulsed with blue light.

"All is ready," Ripley said, indicating the Terrible

Tomes in their cages. "The book whisperer is Obadiah Greene's descendant. It was his power that released you."

Barzak's bloodless lips twisted into a thin smile. His black eyes turned hungrily on Archie. His voice sounded like thunder.

"So, boy, you have the gift. You can unlock the Terrible Tomes and release the dark magic."

Archie turned away. "Never," he cried defiantly.

Arthur Ripley laughed. "We have all the persuasion we need," he said, gesturing at Bramble and Thistle. "He will do anything to save his cousins."

"Then let it begin," Barzak said. The warlock closed his eyes in concentration. Archie heard voices inside the cages. "Release us from our prisons," the voices hissed. "Let us bring our dark magic to the world. Let the Dark Age begin!"

"Patience, my dark brothers and sisters," thundered Barzak. "Long have you waited for this moment—I am restored to you. Together we shall bring a reign of darkness that will last a thousand years."

The warlock turned his gaze on Ripley.

"Unlock the cages!"

Ripley fitted the first silver key into the lock of the first cage and turned it, then moved down the line until he had unlocked all four of the cages containing the Terrible Tomes.

"Are you ready to use your gift to release the Terrible Tomes?" he asked.

"Never!" Archie cried again.

Ripley's face twisted into a crooked smile. "Very well," he said.

He put one hand on Bramble's shoulder and the other on Thistle's and propelled them toward *The Book of Souls*.

"What a shame that your cousin is too foolish to save you," Ripley sneered.

"Do you really think you're going to get away with this?" demanded Archie, trying to stall for time. He was desperately racking his brain to think of something. Anything.

"Who's going to stop me?" laughed Ripley.

"Gideon Hawke," said Archie, trying to sound more confident than he really was.

"That idiot? Don't make me laugh. No, Archie Greene, no knight in shining armor is coming to your rescue."

Something clicked in Archie's mind. A light went on. A knight in shining armor! That's what he needed.

"Funny you should say that!" he said, reaching inside

his bag and producing the glass phial.

"Is that the best you can do?" sneered Ripley. "Do you really think a Popper Stopper is of any use against the Dark Warlock? You are pathetic, Archie Greene."

Archie ignored the taunts. He hurled the glass phial at the flagstone floor.

Ripley was still talking. "Enough. It is time to finish this. Say good-bye to your cousins, Archie Greene!"

There was a loud popping sound behind them. A horse whinnied.

Suddenly, a deep voice boomed from the shadows, "Unhand them, you foul villain! For Archie Greene and the Museum of Magical Miscellany! Charge!"

With a thundering of hooves, Sir Bodwin careered toward the startled Arthur Ripley. Ripley stared in disbelief. Then he let go of Thistle and Bramble and ran into the open cage prepared for *The Book of Souls*.

Sir Bodwin pulled on his reins and his horse reared up. Its front hooves pawed the air, closing the door to the cage. The knight turned his horse around and charged again, this time at Barzak.

"In the name of magic, you shall not prevail this day, you fiend!" he roared. But Archie's relief was short-lived. Barzak raised one clawed hand.

Knight and horse ezaporated with another loud pop.

Barzak's dark eyes flashed with rage. His voice echoed off the walls. "You dare to defy me, book whisperer. For that you will die! But you will serve your purpose first."

Archie felt his hope fading. But in that moment he heard another voice. It was a quiet voice that whispered in his ear. It said, "Have courage. All is not lost. The Tomes are powerful, but they rely on fear. The warlock needs your fear to give him power, too."

Archie remembered *The Little Book of Blessings*. He knew that only he could hear her voice.

"What about my cousins?" he whispered back.

"They must be brave, too. But I will help you. When the warlock tells you to release the magic from the Terrible Tomes, release me instead."

Archie could hear the hissing voices inside the cages. The sound was deafening. He closed his eyes and tried to concentrate.

"Release the Terrible Tomes!" thundered Barzak. "Release my dark brothers and sisters, book whisperer— or your cousins will die!"

What was it that Gran had told him about courage? Real courage wasn't when you felt brave; real courage was when you were frightened but acted anyway. For the first time in his life he really knew what she had meant. His legs felt like jelly, and he was afraid they would fail him. Archie pulled *The Little Book of Blessings* from his pocket. "Stay with me," he whispered. "I need your magic."

Then he screwed up all of his courage.

"I release the magic that lies within
I believe in its power above all things."

He directed his words not at the Terrible Tomes but at the little book in his hand. *The Little Book of Blessings* began to glow, giving off a warm orange light that lit the dark cavern. Archie felt an outpouring of wisdom and courage. And most of all he felt a great surge of hope. The little book felt comforting in his hand, and he felt her magic giving him heart.

"Archie Greene, you have the power to save magic. Believe in yourself," it whispered.

Barzak's black eyes burned with hatred. The warlock raised his voice. "Fool! You think you can disobey me?"

And then suddenly Archie heard a new voice. It was a thin voice, and yet it did not waver.

"I cast you back into the darkness. I command you return to where you came from," it cried. And in that moment Archie recognized his own voice. And as he did, the words became visible, written in fiery green letters that hung in the air. And Archie smelled the aroma of a starlit night.

A look of shock and anger passed across Barzak's face.

"What is this?" he thundered. "How dare you place this feeble magic before the Terrible Tomes? You will pay for this, book whisperer. You and your family are twice cursed."

Barzak loomed over him, but Archie cried out again. "I cast you back into *The Book of Souls*."

The Little Book of Blessings gave one final pulse of light, and Archie knew that it was the very last of her magic. With a sound like thunder, Barzak was sucked back into *The Book of Souls*. Like some grotesque jack-in-the-box, the warlock writhed and twisted as he fought to keep the book open. His black talons ripped at the bindings, and his dark eyes flashed with hatred.

And then, with a scream like a dying animal, his dark robes folded into the pages of the book, and the wrinkled skin of his face and hands disappeared back into the cover. With a final flash of blue light, *The Book of Souls* snapped shut.

Archie heard running footsteps and saw Gideon

THE LAST SECRET   297

Hawke and Morag Pandrama racing toward him. Morag
Pandrama screamed a warning.

Archie whirled around and, to his horror, saw Barzak's grotesque face appear in the cover of *The Book of
Souls* as he made one final attempt to claw his way free of
his prison.

"Archie," cried Gideon Hawke. "The clasp!"

In a single movement, Archie picked up the silver
clasp from the floor and fastened it. With a final exhala-
tion of breath, *The Book of Souls* clicked shut.

CHAPTER 40

Bookends

An hour later, Archie, Bramble, and Thistle were sitting in Quill's, sipping hot chocolate with extra cream and marshmallows.

"Archie, are you sure you are all right?" Gideon Hawke asked, his voice full of concern.

"Yes," said Archie. *The Book of Blessings* lay limp and lifeless in his hand. He looked at Hawke. "She gave us courage when we needed it," he said.

"Yes," breathed Hawke. "It was the last of her magic. You're lucky to be alive. Now you need to rest."

"But there's so much I want to know," Archie protested. "What was von Herring's part in it all?"

"He was working with Arthur Ripley all along. They kidnapped Geoffrey Screech on his way to work. That's why the bookshop was unexpectedly closed the day you and Arabella were supposed to bring your books. We found Screech safe and well at Ripley Hall. He'd been enchanted to keep him quiet, but he will recover."

"And the almanac was a decoy?" Archie asked.

"Yes. It came from the Ripleys' private library and was meant to throw us off the trail of the real Terrible Tome. And when that didn't work, Barzak orchestrated the attacks on the museum, including the flarewolf. He could do that from inside *The Book of Souls*, but he needed a book whisperer to release him from the book."

"Did Arabella know about the plan?"

"No, I think she was just a pawn in the game like you. That girl has many faults, but she probably saved Wolfus's life after the flarewolf attacked him. I suspect Veronica Ripley knew."

"And Rusp?" asked Archie.

"Was working for me," said Hawke. "There was a lot at stake, and I needed to know what was going on. It became even more important when you wouldn't cooperate."

"I see," muttered Archie. "So it wasn't him who dropped the Imagining Glass at the Aisle of White?"

"No," said Hawke. "That was von Herring. He took it from the museum. He had a weakness for magical instruments. He would have taken Dee's pendant as well. I imagine it was von Herring who released the flarewolf from the Popper Stopper later to cause a diversion while he kidnapped your cousins."

"And John Dee's ghost?" Archie asked.

Hawke smiled. "Dee's spirit was finally released from its long vigil," he said. "He is at peace now."

"Good," said Archie. He liked the old man despite all the trouble he had caused for him. He looked up to see Loretta and Woodbine striding purposefully toward them.

"My darling children!" Loretta Foxe trilled. "We came as soon as we heard. Thank heavens you are safe!"

"What ho, young'uns," cried Woodbine, and his large hand gripped Archie's in one of his knuckle-crunching handshakes.

"Well, it's good to see everyone!" Archie smiled. "Well, almost everyone. I wish Gran could be here."

"She's having quite an adventure of her own," said Loretta. "She said she'll tell us about when she gets home."

At that moment, Pink arrived with a large jug of steaming hot chocolate and a plate of cakes.

"Ready for a refill?" she asked. "It's on the house."

Bramble and Thistle cheered loudly. Archie grinned.

Sixty miles away, at the London offices of Folly & Catchpole, Horace Catchpole shifted uncomfortably in his chair. Prudence Folly, the firm's senior partner, was seated opposite him across her desk.

"So let me get this straight," Prudence said, regarding Horace as a falcon might watch a rabbit. "Not only did you forget to deliver the message with the package, you then decided to ignore the firm's rules by opening the scroll and translating it."

Horace nodded. His chin, already low, dropped a bit more.

"Do you have anything to say in your defense?"

Horace took a deep breath. "The thing is," he said, "the scroll was written in a magical language. If I hadn't opened it, they wouldn't have gotten the message at all."

Prudence's face softened. Her thin lips curled into an unaccustomed smile. "I like it, Catchpole! It shows that our special services are still appreciated. Folly and Catchpole has been the Lore firm of choice for the magically minded for centuries! This proves that we still have a place in the world."

Horace smiled brightly. Maybe there was still a chance he'd get a promotion in the spring after all. He hoped that what he was about to say wouldn't ruin everything.

"It was the least I could do," he said. "But there's something I haven't told you."

Prudence sat forward in her chair. "Yes?"

"There's another package for Archie Greene. . . ."

⟶

Inside the Crypt, in the Museum of Magical Miscellany, seven iron cages rested on their marble plinths. The fifth cage was still empty. *The Book of Souls* was finally at rest, but in a separate and very secure place, guarded by one of the Bookend Beasts. The other Terrible Tomes were shut tight.

Inside the glass dome in the Scriptorium, *The Book of Reckoning* was open. The hourglass in its spine gleamed in the light from the single lamp that lit the gloom. The grains of sand inside the hourglass were still. And the Bennu bird quill poised above its open page twitched and danced to the rhythm of life and death.

The other Book of Destiny was closed. But inside *The Book of Prophecy*, a name was being erased . . . and another was being written. . . . But that's another story.

Acknowledgments

Every book is a journey, and this one was long and winding. Thanks are due to some special people without whom Archie and I could not have made it.

~

To Dan, Erin, and Harry (the Cat Suit Club), who were the first to read about Archie's adventures and encouraged me to keep going. And to my sister, Pig, who lived and breathed it with me.

To my agent, Jo Hayes, who along with Paul Moreton and Eddie Bell at Bell Lomax Morton thought there might be something there.

To Leah Thaxton, Rebecca Lee, and everyone at Faber who believed in Archie's magic and took a chance.

To my editors, Alice Swan at Faber and Toni Markiet at HarperCollins, who brought discipline, Chelsea buns, and so much more to transform a rough manuscript into something readable.

To Stuart and Ro for their friendship and indulgence when I should have been writing other things.

Finally, to Sara for her belief and love.